Around the World

## Also by Jerry Labriola

—Murders at Hollings General

—Murders at Brent Institute

—The Maltese Murders

—The Strange Death of Napoleon Bonaparte

—Scent of Danger

—Object of Betrayal

—Deadly Politics

—Global Shadows

—Diamonds and Pirates

—Dangerous Triangle

—The Blue Baron Mystery

—The Saga of Hodge

—Spying for Keeps

—Discovery

—On the Right Track

— Threats and Challenges

— A Better Goal

Coauthored with Dr. Henry Lee

—Famous Crimes Revisited

—Forensic Files

—The Budapest Connection

—Shocking Cases

# Around the World

A NOVEL

By

JERRY LABRIOLA, M.D.

STRONG BOOKS

Strong Books
P.O. Box 715
Avon, CT 06001-0715



First Printing

ISBN 978-1-928782-68-1

Library of Congress Control Number: 2021935263

Published in the United States of America by Strong Books, an imprint of Publishing Directions, LLC



Printed in the United States of America

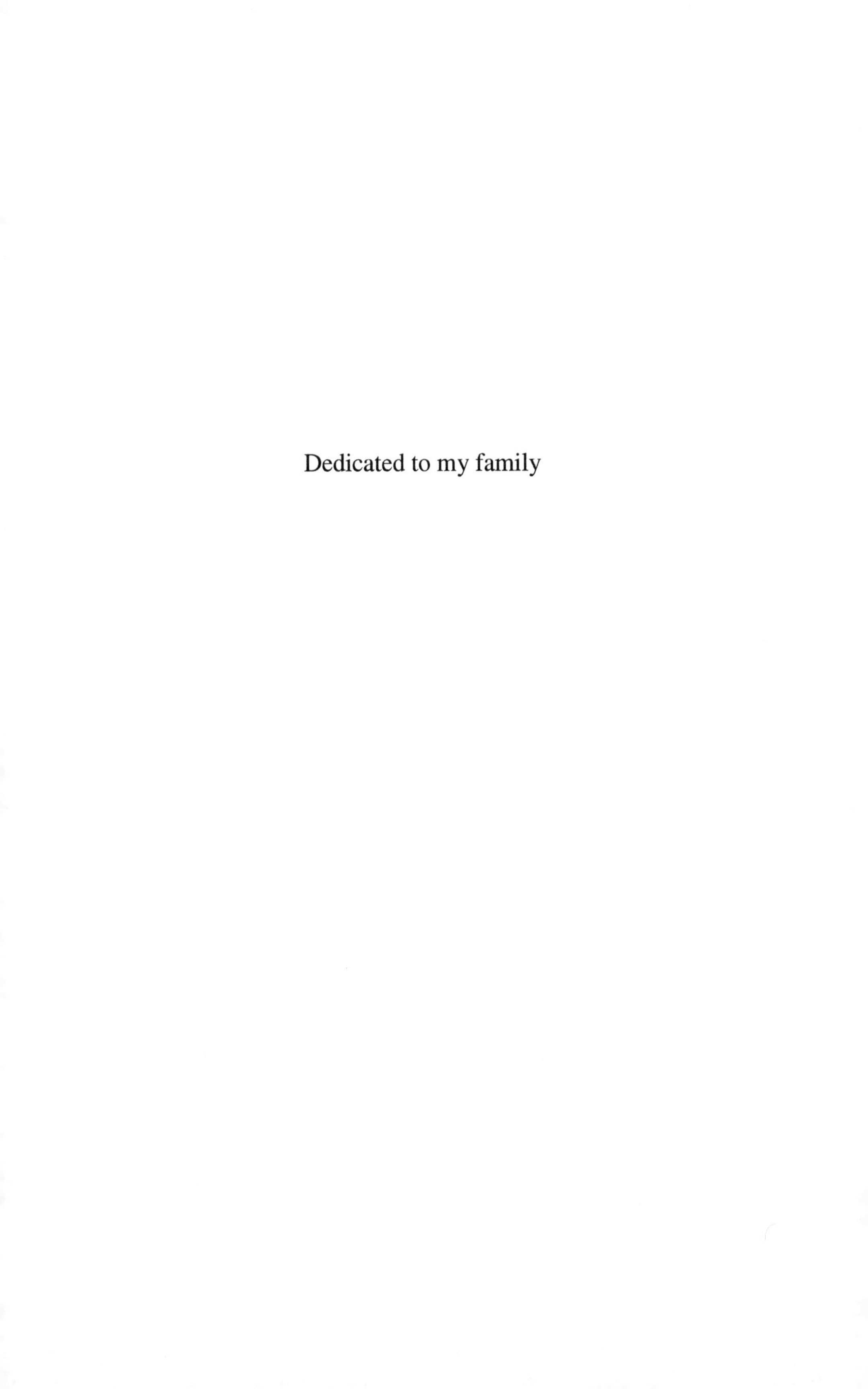

Dedicated to my family

## ACKNOWLEDGMENTS

My sincere thanks to all the Personnel at STRONG BOOKS

# Around the World

## Prologue

This is not a novel — rather, a decade out of one man's life story. A man named Scott — Scott Barlow. It begins in 1953.

He earned a medical degree from Yale but not before he was required to study organic chemistry at Harvard over an eight-week summer period. And it was a reasonable requirement for he'd missed many Yale classes due to travels with its basketball team. He was a team starter and led it in many categories. For several games, three Boston Celtic scouts made notes about him, finally informing him that at 5 feet, 9 inches, he was too short for professional ball.

For Yale though, it was different. In his junior year, he was the leading scorer on a two-week tour of Puerto Rico. He was also the highest scorer in wins over Miami, Pitt, Tampa, Stetson and Vanderbilt. There followed highest scorer in wins over Kansas, Kansas State, Missouri, Iowa State, Colorado, Nebraska and Oklahoma.

He was named an All-Ivy league player and was selected to the little All-American team for players under six-feet tall. For years, his photo appeared in the Encyclopedia Brittanica, demonstrating the technique of dribbling the ball.

So the story unfolds, with highlights from Yale on, his medical pursuits put on hold and time that spanned visits to nearly every city in three world countries: Italy, Greece and France.

His wife, Mary Ellen, also put her own medical practice on hold and gladly joined her husband in his travels.

And his college-day friend, Charlie Banks, was usually at his side.

It didn't take long for them to form a pact: Mary Ellen would remain in the background — reading, writing, napping, visiting libraries, allowing Scott to assume control of the days' agenda. But they would confer regularly. And Scott never expected a Hollywood movie mogul and script writer, Montgomery Lopez, to request the writing of merely a collection of essays. Scott made it 30 in all. There could have been more of them but he settled for his favorite topics.

Scott had written several books but never one with such a weird format, and he knew of no one who had. Would the collection grow too boring to read? He was willing to take a chance that things would turn out fine.

It was a life centered about traveling the world, either offering to help local authorities with local problems and never demanding money for them, for he had purchased a 401-K plan decades before and had lived on hefty sums distributed every January. Or he would simply deliver the essays. His mind sometimes felt tortured, resulting in many changes throughout most days. He might start with a review of maps, a review of destinations, a review of his essays.

He looked the part of an amateur sleuth of sorts. Age 52 and a solid six-foot-five, he kept his dark hair neatly parted on the left side. His eyebrows and thin mustache showed streaks of light gray, while sparkly blue eyes countered a rare smile. Most times though, the eyes seemed to reflect the emotions of his work: uncertainty, suspicion, relief. Even love and hate. And Scott knew it too, believing it to be a handicap. Hence the frequent appearance of dark glasses, even with heavy storms brewing or during prolonged indoor inquiries.

He tried to appear more absorbed in conversation than he really was, checking his surroundings instead. It had become routine for him to be prepared at all times, having practiced the Buddhist concept of mindfulness as a way of managing stress. And, at questionable times, he would feel for two of his pistols, one at his left shoulder, the other in a holster below his right knee.

Many commented on his aversion to overdressing despite the season. He preferred tweed jackets and different shades of charcoal trousers. No hat or overcoat in the winter, just his trademark black scarf and leather gloves. Snow, rain, or a blistery sun were ignored.

His closest friends referred to him as a modern-day Gunga Din, a character developed by Rudyard Kipling and set in British India. “It’s why you write about England and India so often”, they would say in one way or another. And it was certainly one thing on which Montgomery Lopez often devoted his work.

As for the script, what follows is the presentation of each essay, given in the way each was presented. They are:

1 — Napoleon

2 — Mythology

3 — Terrorism

4 — Piracy

5 — Statue of Liberty

6 — Looted treasures

7 — Drama

8 — Motion pictures

9—The Perons

10—Discovery Notes

11 — Tea

12—Eiffel Tower

13—Rock of Gibraltar

14 — London's War Room

15 — Pavarotti

16—Budapest

17—Crime and Comedy Don't Mix

18—Marilyn Monroe

19—President Kennedy Assassination

20—Sacco-Vanzetti

21—Talleyrand

22—Gens de Verite'

23—Diamond Types

24—Volterraio Castle

25—The Hague and Milosevic

26—Cafés in Paris

27—Mystery Books

28—Forensic Science

29—Jack the Ripper

30—Hotel des Invalides

So we march on — 30 chapters, one right after the other — with no stopping in between. And I might feel the need to refer to notes.

How's that sound, Montgomery?

# Chapter 1

## Napoleon

An exiled and dejected Napoleon referred to himself as "Napoleon", not as "I" or "me".

You want to know the treasures of Napoleon? They are enormous, it is true, but in full view. Here they are and, as I explained before, I must refer to notes: the splendid harbor of Antwerp, that of Flushing, capable of holding the largest fleets; the docks and dikes of Dunkirk, of Havre, of Nice; the gigantic harbor of Cherbourg; the harbor works at Venice; the great roads from Antwerp to Amsterdam, from Mainz to Metz, from

Bordeaux to Bayonne, the passes of the Simplon. Of Mont Cenis, of Mont Genevre, of the Corniche that gave four openings through the Alps; in that alone, you might reckon 800 million.

The roads from the Pyrenees to the Alps, from Parma to Spezzia, from Savona to Piedmont; the bridges of Jena, of Austerlitz, of the Arts, of Sevres, of Tours, of Lyons, of Turi, of the Isere, of the Durance, of Bordeau, of Rui; the canal from the Rhine to the Rhone, joining the waters of Holland to the Mediterranean; the canal that joins the Scheldt and the Somme, connecting Amsterdam and Paris; that which joins the Rance and the Vilaine; the canal of the Arles, of Pavia, of the Rhine, the draining of the marches of Bourgoing, of the citentin, of Rochefort; the rebuilding of most of the churches pulled down during the Revolution, the building of new ones.

The construction of many industrial establishments for putting an end to pauperism; the construction of the Louvre; the public graneries, of the Bank, of the canal of the Ourcq; the water system of the city of Paris, the numerous sewers, the Quays, the establishments and monuments of Lyons. Fifty million spent on repairing and improving the Crown residences; sixty million worth of furniture placed in the palaces of France and Holland, at Turin, and Rome; sixty million worth of Crown diamonds, all of it the money of Napoleon; even the Regent, the only missing one of the old diamonds of the Crown of France, purchased from Berlin Jews with whom it was pledged for three million; the Napoleon Museum, valued at more than 400 million. These are monuments to confound calumny. History will relate that all this was accomplished in the midst of continuous wars, without raising a loan, and with the public debt actually decreasing day by day.

Another aspect of Napoleon's life has to do with his many successes but also with his mistakes. As you'll read, the mistakes came about for a certain reason. First off, he had a natural grasp of the essential tactics of war and the art of waging it. He would rattle off aphorisms as if they were golden rules and early on in his career they pretty much were. Like: "A field of battle which the enemy has previously studied and reconnoitered should be avoided", or "March dispersed, fight concentrated:, or "When it is possible to employ thunderbolts, their use should be preferred to that of cannon". And my favorite: "War is an immense art which comprises all others. It is also, like politics, a matter of tact."

Scott formed the words like an evangelistic preacher. "There's almost a pious glory to them," he said, but eventually he blasphemed that glory. Take the first one about reconnoitering. He broke it by attacking Wellington on the Waterloo position even though the Duke had reconnoitered it the year before. And Napoleon knew it. Now then, along about 1812, during the Russian campaign specifically, things began to change. His mechanics of warfare became flawed and that continued until his pitiful at Waterloo three years later. That period was not his finest. For in a way, the real Napoleon ceased to exist. During those two decades and during the Spanish and French campaigns, he violated the classic maneuvers of warfare. Most military experts there are only seven of them. To wit: penetration of the center, envelopment of a single flank, envelopment of both flanks, attack in oblique order, feigned withdrawal, attack from a defensive position, and the indirect approach. But without a doubt, the worst thing he ever said, a dead giveaway that his mind was being altered was:

"I have fought 60 battles and I have learnt nothing that I did not know in the beginning". Can you imagine? Learnt nothing! Have I made my case about the gradual poisoning of one of the greatest military commanders in history — right up there with Alexander and Caesar?

And that brings us to the role of arsenic in Napoleon's life. He and his troops used a small amount as a recreational drug on a regular basis. They had no idea about its cumulative effect. Could it have been slipped to him in larger quantities? How about the wall paper in the room he slept in for years at St. Helena? The paint in the paper had arsenic in it. Could he have been poisoned?

As far as his descent is concerned, he was Italian, being born on the island of Corsica.

Another thing not well known is that three-quarters of all Italian art was brought to the Louvre by him.

# Chapter 2

## Mythology

Myths are older than ancient. They predate recorded history, science and even religion.

They lead us back to a time when the world was young. When people had a connection with the earth and nature — with trees and flowers and hills and seas — unlike anything we ourselves can feel now. In other words, through myths, we can retrace the paths the paths from today's civilized man who lives so far from nature, to man who lived so close to it.

Now the link between myths and nature is only one aspect of what mythology is all about. The general public has, by and large, put its own spin on it — most people dismissing mythology as a pack of silly stories that were, one, made up and two, insignificant.

That's only partly correct, however. Made up? Yes. Insignificant? No.

For myths were explanations made long ago — before science came into vogue — to understand what people were witnessing. Things like lightning, and changes of season, and love, hate and death.

They used gods and heroes, monsters, demons and witches to tell the tales. It was the best that humans could do at the time because they didn't have scientific explanations. Kenneth C. Davis, a great mythology writer, explains that, "natural events, as well as human behavior, came to be understood through tales of gods, goddesses, and heroes. Thunder, earthquakes, eclipses, rain, and the success of crops were all due to the intervention of powerful gods. He goes on to say, "The Greeks believed that, at one time, all the world's evils and problems were trapped inside a box. When this box was opened by the first woman, all the world's misfortunes escaped before she was able to close the lid. They called her Pandora. "Opening Pandora's box."

So myths can be a powerful business. That's one reason they've been around for so long — since the time when the world was full of danger, mystery, and wonder. As if it isn't now!

At times I've talked largely about present-day mysteries, global crime and Napoleon. Now, for what I'd guess you'd call a dramatic change of pace, I'd like to elaborate for just a few minutes on the importance of mythology — something I've always been intrigued with, never fully understood and only recently appreciated its place in the history of civilization.

And I'll confine my remarks to three areas — the impact of myths on our culture, their role in history, and the differences among myths, legends, fables, folktales and fairy tales.

So let's start with #1; the impact of myths — not only those of Greece and Rome — but also those about Norse gods such as Thor and Egyptian gods who inspired the pyramids, for example.

These myths and those from many other civilizations continue to fascinate millions of people, many of whom don't label the whole process as mythology.

Some call it "Going to the Movies". For example, consider: The Lord of the Rings Trilogy, Matrix, Finding Nemo, X-Men, the terminator trilogy, Troy, E.T. (which was really an animated version of Hercules); and above all, Star Wars. All these draw on mythic themes.

Think about this one: There are ancient tales of so-called trickster gods who were greedy, mischievous, and evil—kind of like the joker in Batman.

Often they took animal forms. Like the African Rabbit or Native American Coyote. Sounds like Bugs Bunny and his nemesis Wiley Coyote to me!

It's not just the entertainment industry that's capitalized on myth. How about Halloween — a modern version of an ancient mythical celebration?

In fact, many of the trappings of Christmas, including Christmas trees wreaths, mistletoe holly and ivy are borrowed from ancient traditions of northern Europe. The evergreen symbolized the hope for new life in the dead of winter.

To get another gauge of the impact of myths, check the calendar. The names of all the days and months derive from Greek, Roman and Norse mythology.

Check the planets in our solar system: all except the earth are named for Roman gods.

Check our language: loaded with words from our mythic past: do you buy books from Amazon.com? Are you wearing a pair of Niles? How about words like panacea, panic, hypnosis, leprechaun, typhoon, hurricane? Myths surround us in literature, in pop culture, in our language.

Next, #2: History. Myths also play a serious role here. In wartime Japan, for example, they were the source of the national Shinto religion. The Japanese emperor Hirohito was supposedly descended from a Shinto sun goddess. Devotion to the emperor led to the use of notorious kamikaze pilots with their dynamite-laden planes and their suicide crashes into U.S. warships. It was a myth/religion that drove those young men — and an entire nation.

Even in the Napoleonic era, King Louis the 16th thought he had divine authority. His was a reign that was generally considered oppressive, and which played a role in the outbreak of the French Revolution.

Of course, it doesn't end there, as a certain history has shown. I refer to 9/11. The notion of dying a martyr's death and gaining entrance to a paradise with the promise of virgins is an enticing idea that continues to drive terrorists who strap explosives to their bodies, drive cars filled with explosives, or fly hijacked jets into buildings.

They're motivated by beliefs whose roots stretch back centuries. The idea of warriors gaining access to paradise through early death is certainly not exclusive to any one mythology or faith. We might even say that one person's myth is another person's religion.

The history of myths, in other words, goes hand in hand with the history of civilization. Stop and think about ancient civilization.

What does it mean? The wheel. Writing. Bronze. Glass. Fireworks. Paper. Noodles. In-door plumbing. Beer.

These are only a few of the pleasant and delightful creations devised by the ancient civilizations of Egypt, China, Greece, India, Rome, and others. These civilizations also gave us astronomy, democracy, and philosophy.

Now you're probably thinking, "Wait a minute. All you're doing is listing various discoveries."

Yes, but here's the important point. These same ancients invented the myths that grew hand in hand with the discoveries of their civilizations, making it impossible to separate one from the myths from history itself.

So while the importance of myths may seem less obvious than that of the wheel writing, or a mug of beer, these old stories are still a dominant force in our lives today. They remain alive in our literature, our language, theatre, dreams, psychology and various religions.

Okay. All I've said so far has been about impact and history. Now just a word about the meaning of "myth". It's derived from the Greek word "mythox", meaning "story". It was Plato who coined the word "mythology" more than 2,000 years ago.

To say it in a different way: myths began so that humans could explain and describe the world they could see as well as the world they only imagined existed.

That is the world they couldn't see.

I'm talking about long before science envisioned the Big Bang. Long before philosophers reasoned or sought enlightenment. Long before Jesus walked the shores of the Sea of Galilee. Long before there was bible or a Koran. Long before Darwin proposed natural selection. Long before we could know the age of a rock, and long before men walked on the moon.

They explained:

— How earth was created.

— Where life came from.

— Why the stars shine at night and the seasons change.

— Why there is sex.

— Why there is evil.

— Why people die and where they go when they do.

In short, myths are a very human way to explain everything.

Finally, #3: What are the differences among myths, legends, fables, folktales, and fairy tales? They're not the same.

— Myths usually involve gods—supernatural beings who actually control events in the natural world.

— Legends, on the other hand, are really an early form of stories about historical figures, usually humans, not gods. Most Americans, for example, know the story of George Washington and the cherry tree. A legend.

— Fables are simple, usually brief, fictitious stories, typically with a moral. In many fables, the moral is usually told at the end, in the form of a proverb. Often, they feature animals that speak and act like human beings, as in the most famous examples—those attributed to Aesop in Aesop's Fables.

— Stories like The Tortoise and the Hare, in which slow and steady wins the race. That's the moral. Or The Grasshopper and the Ant in which a fun-loving but lazy grasshopper plays while the ant dutifully stores away food for the winter. There's a moral there, too.

Another famous collection is Grimm's Fairy Tales which include Hansel and Gretel, Little Red Riding Hood, Snow White, and Sleeping Beauty. Many of these were drawn from older, mythic sources.

So it is that the myths of every culture include all of the other types of stories—that is, legends, fables, folk, and fairy tales. It's really a neat arrangement—one that's given us a sweeping and stimulating view of the world.

Before ending, I thought I'd touch again on my hero, Napoleon Bonaparte and on French history. It might get a bit technical but it's the way I've handled it in all my writings. The important dates are 1799, 1800, 1803, 1804, and 1806. After having imposed a military dictatorship on France by coup d'etat in 1799, Napoleon strengthened his position. He adopted the Constitution of the Year VIII which gave executive power to a college of three consuls and legislative power to four assemblies. He broke the Jacobin opposition (to which the attempted crime of Rue Saint-Nicaise was attributed), organized the administration and the economy, began judicial reforms, and encouraged religious calm. I feel that he never received enough credit for his strong feelings about religion. Elsewhere, he imposed peace on Austria which had been beaten at Marengo, and signed with her the Treaty of Luneville. This was also about the time he obliged an isolated England to sign the Peace of Amiens.

# Chapter 3

## Terrorism

Terrorism is, in the broadest sense, the use of indiscriminate violence as a means to create terror among masses of people, or fear to achieve a religious or political aim. It is used in this regard primarily to refer to violence during peacetime or in the context of war against non-combatants—mostly civilians and neutral military personnel. The terms "terrorist and "terrorism" originated during the French Revolution pf the late 18$^{th}$ century but gained mainstream popularity in the 1970s in news reports and books covering the conflicts in Northern Ireland, the Basque Country and Palestine. The increased use of suicide attacks from the 1980s onward was typified by the 9/11 attacks in New York City and Washington, D.C. in 2001.

There are different definitions of terrorism. It's a charged term. It is often used with the connotation of something that is morally wrong. Government and non-state groups us the term to abuse or denounce opposing groups. Varied political organizations have been accused of using terrorism to achieve their objectives. These organizations include right right-wing and left-wing political organizations, nationalist groups, religious groups, revolutionaries and ruling governments.

Legislation declaring terrorism a crime has been adopted in many states. When terrorism is perpetrated by nation states, it is not considered terrorism by the state perpetrating it, making legality a largely grey-area issue. There is no consensus as to whether or not terrorism should be considered a war crime.

There are over 109 different definitions of terrorism. Experts disagree about whether terrorism is wrong by definition or just wrong as matter of fact. They disagree about whether it should be defined in terms of its aims, or its methods, or both, or neither. They even disagree about whether or not states can perpetrate terrorism.

In November 2004, Kofi Annan, Secretary General of the United Nations described terrorism as any act intended to cause death or serious bodily harm to civilians or non-combatants with the purpose of intimidating a population or compelling a government or an international organization to do or abstain from doing an act.

The international community has been slow to formulate a universally agreed upon, legally binding definition of this crime. These difficulties arise from the fact that the term "terrorism" is politically and emotionally charged.

A brief to the Australian parliament stated, "The international community has never succeeded in developing an accepted comprehensive definition of terrorism. During the 1970s and 1980s, the United Nations' attempts to define the term floundered, mainly due to differences of opinion between various members about the use of violence in the context over national liberation and self-liberation."

Since 1994, the United States General Assembly has repeatedly condemned terrorist attacks, using the following political description of it: "Criminal acts intended or calculated to provoke a state of terror in the public, or to a group of persons for political purposes."

International terrorism means activities with the following three characteristics: One — Involve violent acts or acts dangerous to human life that violate federal or state law. Two — Appear to be intended to intimidate or coerce a civilian population; to influence the policy of a government by intimidation or coercion; or to affect the conduct of a government by mass destruction, assassination, or kidnapping. And Three — Occur primarily outside the territorial jurisdiction of the U.S., or transcend national boundaries in terms of the means by which they are accomplished, the persons they appear intended to intimidate or coerce, or the locale in which their perpetrators operate or seek asylum.

Since 9/11, there has been a five-fold increase in deaths from terrorist attacks. The majority of incidents over the past several years can be tied to groups with a religious agenda.

Before 2000, it was nationalist separatist organizations such as the IRA and Chechen rebels who were behind most attacks. The number of incidents from nationalist separatist groups has remained stable in the years since, while religious extremism has grown. The prevalence of Islamic groups in Iraq, Afghanistan, Pakistan, Nigeria and Syria is the main driver behind these trends.

Four of the terrorist groups that have been most active since 2001 are Boko Haram, Al Qaeda, the Taliban and ISIL. These groups have been most active in Iraq, Afghanistan, Pakistan, Nigeria, and Syria. Eighty percent of all deaths from terrorism occurred in one of these five countries.

# Chapter 4

## Piracy

A pirate is a person who attacks and robs ships. Such robbers have also been called freebooters, ladrones, pickaroons, and sea rovers. Pirates differ from sea raiders known as privateers. Pirates were not licensed by any nation but privateers were licensed by a particular nation during wartime to attack enemy ships. Therefore, privateers were generally not considered pirates

Pirates have robbed ships and raided coastal towns since ancient times. The greatest period of pirate attacks, or "piracy", occurred from the 1500s through the 1700s on the Mediterranean and Caribbean seas. The most famous pirates of this age included Henry Morgan, Blackbeard and William Kidd. Most pirates were men, but a few women took on a pirate role.

Widespread piracy no longer exists, but attacks have occurred in some areas. In the 1980s for example, pirates carried out numerous attacks against Cambodian and Vietnamese refugees in the Gulf of Thailand.

Regarding how pirates lived, they became them for various reasons. Sometimes, the harsh conditions of life at sea led honest seamen to desert or mutiny their ships. These men often turned to piracy to survive. Other sought riches or adventure. Many privateers drifted into piracy when wars between nations ended.

Legend, fiction and motion pictures have helped create an exciting, romantic picture of pirates. A typical pirate is portrayed as a fierce-looking man with a beard. Most carried several kinds of weapons such as a pistol, daggers, a boarding ax, and a short, curved sword called a cutlass. He is sometimes handsomely dressed.

In real life, however, most pirates led miserable lives. They were often drunk and quarrelsome. Many died of wounds or disease. Some were shot or marooned by their own crews or captured and sentenced to death by authorities.

In spite of their unlawful way of life, most pirate crews developed rules and regulations to govern their ships. Crew members elected a captain and other officers and had a code of punishment for breaking agreements. They also developed pay scales to determine each person's share of the booty.

Until about 1700, pirate ships flew a red banner called "The Bloody Flag". They then began using flags that pictured such objects as skeletons, flaming swords and hourglasses. The most popular of the new pirate flags showed a white skull and crossbones on a black background. This symbol became known as the "Jolly Roger".

Ships involved in trade carried weapons in case of attack. But a pirate crew usually outnumbered the other crew and could defeat it in hand-to-hand combat after coming aboard. Pirates seized trading ships by first maneuvering their vessel next to the ship. They boarded by using hooks and ropes to keep the ships together.

Besides robbing ships, pirates also attacked towns. In the towns, they murdered innocent people and took prisoners. The pirates held some captives for ransom and enslaved others. They sometimes tortured prisoners to get information about treasure. There is little evidence that they made their victims "walk the plank".

# Chapter 5

## Statue of Liberty

The statue is as tall as the length of a football field. Etched in a bronze plaque in its pedestal since 1903 is a sonnet written by American poet Emma Lazarus. It says in part:

Not like the brazen giant of Greek fame
With conquering limbs astride from land to land,
Here at our sea-washed sunset gates shall stand
A mighty woman with a torch, whose flame

Is the imprisoned lightning, and her name
Mother of Exiles. From her beacon hand
Glows world-wide welcome; her mild eyes command
The air-bridged harbor that twin cities frame.
"Keep, ancient lands, your storied pomp!" cries she
With silent lips. Give me your tired, your poor,
Your huddled masses yearning to breathe free.
The wretched refuse of your teeming shore.
Send these, the homeless, tempest-tossed to me,
I lift my lamp beside the golden door.

And so it was.

But no matter how you identify the statue, she still embodies all the freedoms we have in America:

Freedom of the press

Freedom of speech

Freedom of assembly

And, of course, freedom of religion.

The statue was built piece by piece in Paris in 1885 to commemorate the Declaration of Independence. It was then shipped to the U.S. in 241 crates and assembled at its present site in New York harbor.

Periodically, we should think of those millions who came here to fulfill a dream — really.

But by the same token, we should consider what they gave in return. They became an amalgam of what the U.S. comprises — of what many refer to as "the fabric of our society".

They arrived from every port in Europe: from Bremen and Antwerp and Rotterdam and Lisboa. From Lehavre and Liverpool and Copenhagen and Constantinople and Fiume and Naples.

The came because they knew for sure that they'd find liberty — the most powerful idea the world has ever known.

Men and women have spoken it in unparalleled acts of courage — even today — as we read about it incessantly.

And liberty — in a special way — belongs to America. It's been identified with us through the years — because here, it's been tested over and over again.

And here, it's sustained to a degree unique in the history of mankind.

And that's why so many came to U.S. shores rather than to others.

Twenty million of them — and if you include their descendants, you have a figure of about 120 million who passed through Ellis Island and waved to Miss Liberty when they arrived.

That represented 40% of our population, though I daresay the percentage was even higher in some states — perhaps double.

And upon arrival, they of course found great differences in wealth and influence.

But they quickly learned that every person and every family could rise as high as talent and drive and sacrifice permitted.

Toss in some luck if you wish and — yes — the good grace of God.

But even if you put all of that aside — they understood that no one could fall below the level of human dignity.

As one gentleman put it, "In the United States the president is 'Mister' and I am 'Mr', too".

And when they came, oh how they labored:

Italians and Russian Jews worked in the sweat shops of Manhattan's lower east side.

Irish and Germans and Poles and Swedes helped lay rails west across their new country.

But that was just the beginning, for we all recognize some of the dreams that followed:

A hat maker's son from Minsk becomes a university professor.

A poor farmer's son from Kerry becomes a war correspondent.

The son of Polish immigrants becomes a famous surgeon.

And here in America, again and again, many individuals rose from factory floor to front office.

Or left a crowded tenement for a home of their own.

Or worshipped in peace.

Or watched their children graduate from college.

Or served their communities.

Or all of these things.

These were grand achievements — lasting achievements — and they were made in America.

Of equal importance, immigrants remade America. It's inconceivable to imagine the United States without the genius, the artistry, and the thought which they brought to this land.

We listen to their music.

We read their books.

We watch their plays and movies.

Our food, our language, and even our humor have been shaped by them.

And most profoundly, the very texture of our society — from New York to Los Angeles, and from Chicago to New Orleans — has become a single mosaic of many cultures. A place which Walt Whitman rightly described as, "not merely a nation, but a teeming of nations".

These then were our immigrants — our mothers and fathers and grandparents and maybe some of you.

They arrived — they became citizens — they were absorbed, and they gave back a piece of themselves to the new land they cherished.

Liberty and United States citizenship are synonymous but all too often they're taken for granted.

Think about it. There's no force or mandate here. We don't live in a police state.

On our soil, no one regularly taps you on the shoulder and demands to see your papers. There are no such papers here.

A family may move freely from coast to coast without registering with the authorities. There ARE no authorities to take such registration.

Nor has this ever been the land of a midnight knock on the door — when armed militia would haul you away.

In America, you may mimeograph a handbill, run for president, become a drifter, or worship the sun.

You may copyright your laundry list, denounce your elected officials, change your name, read palms, burn books, put ketchup on cottage cheese, raise cane or corn — and chances are good that no one in authority will even raise an eyebrow.

And so — to wind things down: it was in this setting of freedom, and liberty, and opportunity that our forbearers came.

Where American citizenship thrives as the expression of voluntary acts — of free people in a free society.

And therein lies the strength and spirit of this nation.

May God bless America.

# Chapter 6

## Looted treasures

Some antiquities are rumored to be cursed. But those stolen and sold do leave a trail of lawsuits — and sometimes bodies — in their wake.

The looting and illicit export of art treasures is not a new problem.

They've happened whenever there have been armed conflicts during which victorious troops plundered churches, temples, and other buildings. Germany carried out massive looting in World War II.

By the start of the 21st century, the trade in massive antiquities had become so huge, it was worth billions of dollars each year and was the biggest international crime outside of drug and arms trafficking.

When a piece is stolen, the consequences for scholars might be tragic, because essential information about the piece — where it was found, what else was with it — could be lost forever.

In recent years, numerous American museums — including the Metropolitan Museum of Art in New York, Boston's Museum of Fine Arts and the Getty in Los Angeles — have been forced to return antiquities to their host countries. These include the famed krater (wine bowl) dating from 515 BC.

Probably the most dramatic case of looted antiquities concerns the notorious Sevso treasure, a magnificent cashe of late Ropman silver dating from the 41st or 45th century AD and comprising inlaid platters and bowls which were unearthed in the late 1970s. The finder was later found hanged in a cellar and two of his friends died under unexplained circumstances. The silver — contained in a giant copper cauldron that he had buried in the cellar — had disappeared.

Two or three years ago, Syria returned relics to Iraq; France returned items to Burkina Faso, a republic in West Africa; and Denmark repatriated relics to China. Both Italy and the Vatican returned parts of the looted Parthenon to Greece.

Also around then, in the Ethiopian town of Axum, tens of thousands turned out for the unveiling of a treasured obelisk that was taken by Italian troops in 1937, but returned after lengthy negotiations between Rome and Addis Ababa.

During World War II,, European Jews were victimized twice. Not only were that victims of the Holocaust, but they were also victims of Nazi officials who stole from them. Homes were invaded and stores plundered. The trains came into Auschwitz, a concentration camp in Poland, and as the people stepped off the train, not only were they separated from their families, but they were ordered to place to [place their belongings into baskets — clothes in one, books in another, jewelry in another, gold in another.

Everything was separated. From wedding rings to gold fillings from teeth, the Jews' possessions were then melted into gold and sent to Switzerland where Germany acquired hard currency to carry on the war effort, As the Nazi swept across Europe, they confiscated gold from each country they invaded. The money contained in the Swiss bank accounts from both the central banks of Europe and Holocaust victims is said to be billions in dollars. As the Nazis shipped valuables to Switzerland, they made extensive use of the safe deposit boxes there. American documents have related that there are hundreds of millions of dollars in bank vaults, composed of jewelry, securities, artwork assets, and valuables. Some of it was returned — most was not.

# Chapter 7

## Drama

Drama is an art form that tells a story through the speech and actions of the characters in the story.  Most drama is performed by actors who impersonate the characters before an audience in a theater.

Although drama is a form of literature, it differs from other literary forms in the way it is presented. For example, a novel is also tells a story involving characters. But a novel tells its story through a combination of dialogue and narrative, and is complete on the printed page.

Most drama achieves its greatest effect when it is performed. Some critics believe that a written script is not really a play until it has been acted before an audience.

Drama probably gets most of its effectiveness from its ability to give order and clarity to human experience. The basic elements of drama — feelings, desires, conflicts, and reconciliations — are the major ingredients of human experience. In real life, these emotional experiences often seem to be a jumble of unrelated impressions. In drama, however, the playwright can organize these experiences into understandable patterns. The audience sees the material of real life presented in meaningful form — with the unimportant omitted and the significant emphasized.

No one knows exactly how or when drama began, but nearly every civilization has had some form of it. Drama may have developed from ancient religious ceremonies that were performed to win favor from the gods. In these ceremonies, priests often impersonated supernatural beings or animals, and sometimes imitated such actions as hunting. Stories grew up around some rites and lasted after the rites themselves had died out. These myths may have formed the basis of drama.

Another theory suggests that drama originated in choral hymns of praise sung at the tomb of a dead hero. At some point, a speaker separated from the chorus and began to act out deeds in the hero's life. This acted part gradually became more elaborate, and the role of the chorus diminished. Eventually the stories were performed as plays, their origins forgotten.

According to a third theory, drama grew out of a natural love of storytelling. Stories told around campfires re-created victories in the hunt or in battle, or the feats of dead heroes. These stories developed into dramatic retellings of the events.

Among the many forms of Western drama are (1) tragedy, (2) serious drama, (3) melodrama, and (4) comedy. Many plays combine forms. Modern dramatists often disregard these categories and create new forms.

Tragedy maintains a mood that emphasizes the play's serious intention, though there may be moments of comic relief. Such plays feature a tragic hero, an exceptional yet flawed individual who is brought to disaster and usually death. The hero's fate raises questions about the meaning of existence, the nature of fate, morality and social or psychological relationships. Aristotle identified the emotional effect of tragedy as the "catharsis of pity and fear".

Serious drama, which developed out of tragedy, became established in the 1800's. It shares the serious tone and often the serious purpose of tragedy and, like tragedy, it concentrates on unhappy events. But serious drama can end happily, and its heroes are less imposing and more ordinary than the tragic hero. Serious drama is sometimes viewed as tragedy's modern successor.

Melodrama involves a villain who initiates actions that threaten characters with whom the audience is sympathetic. Its situations are extreme and often violent, though endings are frequently happy. Melodrama portrays a world in which good and evil are clearly distinguished. As a result, almost all melodramas have a sharply defined, oversimplified moral conflict.

Comedy tries to evoke laughter, often by exposing the pretensions of fools and rascals. Comedy usually ends happily. But even in the midst of laughter, comedy can raise surprisingly serious questions. Comedy can be both critical and playful, and it may arouse various responses. For example, satiric comedy tries to arouse scorn, while romantic comedy tries to arouse joy.

Farce is sometimes considered a distinct dramatic form, but it is essentially a type of comedy. Farce uses ridiculous situations and broad physical clowning for its humorous effects.

# Chapter 8

## Motion Pictures

Motion pictures is a series of images recorded on film or tape that appear to move when played through a film projector or a videotape player. Also known as movies, film, or cinema, the motion picture is one of the most popular forms of art and entertainment throughout the world. It is also a major source of information.

Every week, millions of people go to the movies. Many millions more watch movies that are broadcast on television or are played back on a videotape or DVD player.

But movies are much more than just entertainment. The motion picture is a major art form, as are, for example, painting and drama. Artists express themselves by using paint and dramatists; and dramatists by using words. Filmmakers express their ideas through a motion picture camera. By using the camera in different ways, the filmmaker can express different points of view. A filmmaker may film scenes for a picture in a desert, on a mountain, or in a large city. Filmmakers can also fill scenes from different angles. Later, through a process called "editing", they can select the angle that most effectively expresses a dramatic point. Through editing, the filmmakers can also show events happening at the same time in different places.

Silent movies established the power of film. Silent stars such as Charlie Chaplin gained worldwide fame. The 1925 soviet classic, "The Battleship Potemkin" showed how film could be used as propaganda. It featured a scene of civilians being massacred by their government.

The musical fantasy,"The Wizard of Oz", has been an audience favorite since it was released in 1939. Judy Garland, its young heroine, became one of the most popular stars in movie history.

# Chapter 9

## Eva and Juan Peron

Certain reports date back to the days of Eva Peron. That she offered asylum to some heinous Nazis. Some of the latter hid there in Argentina, changing their names and faking a normal life — with her help. But others remained criminals in many ways.

She had a successful career in radio, movies and the theater and soon won the affection of the Argentine people. Born in 1919 as an illegitimate child, she became a prostitute to survive and to obtain those roles. She also became a mistress to army officers. And due to her ties with prominent Nazis, it is alleged that she paved the way for the prevalence and fascism across Latin America.

Known as “Evita” by her adoring followers, it is claimed that because of her ties to Nazis, Switzerland would come into the equation. She and a longtime friend and Swiss diplomat were to arrange a relationship between Argentina and important leaders of Europe. But there was a parallel mission behind the high-profile trip, one that contributed to a half-century of violent extremism in Latin America.

This new evidence of Evita’s cozy ties with prominent Nazis corroborates the long-held suspicion that she and her husband, Gen. Juan Peron, laid the groundwork for a bloody resurgence of fascism cross Latin America in the 1970s and 80s.

Besides blemishing the Evita legend, evidence threatens to inflict more damage on Switzerland’s image for plucky neutrality. The international banking center is still staggering from disclosures about wartime collaboration with Adolph Hitler and Swiss profiteering off his Jewish victims. The archival records indicate that Swiss assistance to Hitler's henchmen didn't stop with the collapse of the Third Reich.

During World War II, General Peron, a populist military leader, made no secret of his sympathies for Mussolini's Italy and Hitler's Germany.

Even as the Third Reich crumbled in the spring of 1945, Peron remained a pro-fascist stalwart, making available more than 1,000 blank passports for Nazis fleeing Europe.

With Europe in chaos and the Allies near victory, tens of thousands of ranking Nazis dropped out of sight, tried to mix in with common refugees and began plotting escapes from Europe to Argentina across clandestine "ratlines".

By 1946, the first wave of defeated fascists was settling into new Argentine homes. The country also was rife with rumors that the thankful Nazis had begun to repay Peron by bankrolling his campaign for presidency, which he won with his stunning wife by his side.

In 1947, Peron was living in Argentina's presidential palace and was hearing pleas from thousands of other Nazis desperate to flee Europe. The stage was set for one of the most troubling boatlifts in human history.

Archival records reveal that Eva Peron stepped forward to serve as Gen. Peron's personnel emissary to this Nazi underground. Already , Evita was an Argentine legend.

As she climbed the social ladder, lover to lover, she built up deep resentments toward the traditional elites. And as a mistress to army officers, Evita fashioned herself as the "queen of the poor", and the protector of those she called ,"mis descamisados" — "my shirtless ones". She created a foundation to help the poor buy items from toys to houses. But her charity extended, too, to her husband's Nazi allies.

# Chapter 10

## Discovery Notes and Dreams

These are interchangeable. It seems that whenever Scott's mind enters a dream state — mostly at night but even during a lazy afternoon — the dream get wrapped around a series of both related and unrelated issues. He calls them, "Discovery Notes". Some he recognizes; others he doesn't. Some he's delighted to encounter; others are plain frightening. And he wasn't at all sure why many items were listed. They seemed to come out of nowhere, having little meaning in his life. These were the circumstances he was about to face. But then, he would reason — dreams are dreams and mysterious words and phrases are likely to pop up. Also, in a strange way, his dreams might even include events that hadn't even yet take place. Would there simply crossing his mind make them fair game for future dreams? If so, could he learn from them?

With thoughts still churning in his head, Scott next dreamed of the Discovery Notes, including what he had previously jotted down. It took him well over an hour to ensure that they were all-inclusive. He actually looked forward to doing so because it was to be the solution to the problem he'd face: how could he interrupt his plans in order to write a novel? There was just so much time in a day and he was ready for it to come on:

Tired of travel unless for different reason. Will not give up karate work. Want to search for "the progress and legitimacy of religion". To write book about it. To visit with a variety of people, like Fabio Calderone, Thatcher Drinkwater, Joe Gomez, Juan Saltanban, maybe others. Then to countries and places like Germany, France , Gibraltar, Switzerland, Japan. Considering investigation of cruise lines. Will continue to make notes like these during travels. Then use them later in writing the book. Should be non-fiction. Met with Guy Martin of Herald Tribune. Writes weekly column. Lunch with him at Bonfiore Restaurant. He inquires about Sylvie. He proposes additional purpose to trips: combine churches and pastors with related criminal activity. Digital world now. Says some pastors accept prostitutes provided by mobsters. Suspicious-looking guy spotted at nearby table. Eye-to-eye visits recommended. Leon Cassell mentioned (Verite). Also JBCC and pilot friend, Ansel Stone. He will provide limo for anywhere. Am allowed to be armed with pistols during flights. Rainy downpour when leaving. Reading of religion and Napoleon and attending church services through the years. Accumulated snippets. The "List of Five". Napoleon's quote regarding priests. Arrive home. Description of yard. Imagining what inside looks like. Dial Sylvie. She agrees with Guy. "Cover for Crime". About the Mafia. About Fabio Calderone form Calabria He spent 13 years in Chicago. Great friends. Was once an expert on fronts. Now is barber replacing murdered Rocco Stratta. Phone call to Fabio. "In and out visit" proposed. General reasons for upcoming visit to Italy. Charlie Banks and Thatcher Drinkwell mentioned. Also histarians, not historians. Munching on crackers. Sylvie calls. Charlie best possible bodyguard. His description. Leave for Calabria. Charlie naps. Reading about past visits to Elba and its Volterraio Castle. Dwelling upon Fabio and Thatcher regarding religion and Napoleon. Thatcher's histarians mentioned again along with where Napoleon was born. Calabria description. The airport (Lamezia). To begin writing notes during upcoming sailing. Arrival at barber shop. Fabio sitting in chair before mirror. His description. Says he knows and likes Drinkwell. The latter's loose-leaf binders. Mention of preliminary hearings, then countries to be visited. Few notes made. Fabio says dons of both eras believed Napoleon and religion closely related. Fabio considers various religions, fronts and cruise lines. Gunshots heard. Discovery of our car's shot out tires. Decision made to stay the night. Fabio's guns. Assured of cots in rear room. Dinner at LaFortuna Restaurant.Quiet  talk. Beat-up black car seen through window. Depart for airport in morning.

# Chapter 11

## Tea

Tea comes in three basic types: black, oolong and green. All three types derive from the leaves of a plant that is a member of the evergreen family. It's a family that thrives in semi-tropical climates. Differences in local weather patterns, soil conditions and elevation produce more than 3,000 different varieties. By definition, herbal tea is not really tea at all, but offers similar enjoyment.

Black tea is produced by air-drying newly harvested leaves, crushing them to begin oxidation, which changes the color of the leaves to brown and then black, and drying them under high temperatures to seal in the flavor. Nearly 92% of tea that is consumed is a combination of black tea varieties.

Oolong tea undergoes the cam process as black tea, but the oxidation time is much briefer This results in a delicate flavor, typically fruity and mellow.

Green tea is produced by steaming the leaves shortly after harvest. Because steaming prevents oxidation, green tea tastes more like a raw tea plant than black or oolong. It has a delicate color, which ranges from almost clear to gold to shimmering, transparent green. This category includes Gunpowder tea which is rolled into little balls that expand in hot water. Worldwide, 6% of consumed tea is green.

Herbal tea is actually an "infusion" made from flowers, fruits, spices and, of course, herbs rather than from the leaves of the tea plant. Packaged and brewed like real tea, herbal teas contain no caffeine and yield an array of delicate, subtle flavors. Examples are Chamomile, Peppermint, Lemon Grass and the popular Hibiscus.

Tea is nearly the world's most popular beverage, second only to water in international consumption. In fact, over one and a half billion cups of tea are consumed daily across the globe.

A tea tour of China, Great Britain and the U.S. might now be appropriate:

According to legend, tea was discovered in China in 2737 B.C. when a few errant tea leaves blew into water boiling in the kettle of an emperor.

In Great Britain, tea is more than just a drink. It's a way of life, often starting with a traditional "early morning cuppa" before rising out of bed. The remainder of the day revolves around tea, from "elevenses", a mid-morning tea break, to the now famous "afternoon tea" that began in the Court of Anna, 7$^{th}$ Duchess of Bedford.

Regarding America, when early colonists arrived, they had brought tea with them, intertwining the nation's history with tea from the very start. By the end of the 18$^{th}$ century, tea was so popular that when England levied a heavy tax on its import, angry patriots dumped newly arrived tea into the Boston harbor. This sign of rebellion, ironically called the "Boston Tea Party", triggered a series of events that ultimately led to the Declaration of Independence in 1776. Americans have since contributed greatly to the fables history of tea, inventing both the tea bag and iced tea.

# Chapter 12

## Eiffel Tower

An object of discord and fascination, the Eiffel Tower never fails to impress. Enriched by a history full of new developments, what follows presents all you might hear about it.

It was at the 1889 Exposition Universelle, the date that marked the 100th anniversary of the French Revolution, that a great competition was launched in the Journal Officiel.

The first digging work started on the 26th of January, 1887. Gustave Eiffel was in charge. It was not his only creation. This enthusiastic and true genius was able to go beyond his own limits to bequeath monuments such as the dome on the Nice Observatory, or the metallic structure of the Statue of Liberty, or the Bordeaux railway bridge.

The tower is located in the 7th arrondissement of Paris. Upon the German occupation in 1940, the lift cables were cut by the French people. The tower was closed to the public during the occupation and the lifts were not repaired until 1946.

In 1940, German soldiers had to climb the tower to hoist a swastika-centered Reichskriegsflagge, but the flag was so large it blew away just a few hours later and was replaced by a smaller one.

Upon visiting Paris, Hitler chose to stay on the ground. When the Allies were nearing Paris in August, 1944, Hitler ordered the military governor of Paris to demolish the tower along with the rest of the city. The governor disobeyed the order. On June 25, before the Germans had been driven out of Paris, the German flag had been replaced with a Tricolor by two men from the French Naval Museum, who narrowly beat three men who had lowered the Tricolor in 1940 when Paris fell to the Germans.

A fire started in the television transmitter in 1956, damaging the top of the tower. Repairs took a year. In 1957, the present radio aerial was added to the top. In 1954, the Eiffel Tower was officially declared to be an historical monument by the Minister of Cultural Affairs. A year later, an additional lift was installed in the north pillar.

According to interviews, in 1967, the Montreal mayor negotiated a secret agreement with Charles de Gaulle for the tower to be dismantled and temporarily relocated to Montreal to serve as a landmark and tourist attraction during Expo 67. The plan was allegedly, vetoed by the company operating the tower out of fear that the French government would refuse permission for the tower to be restored in its original location.

# Chapter 13

## The Rock

The Rock of Gibraltar is a limestone promontory of the British overseas territory of Gibraltar. The territory has a population of about 30 thousand. Most residents are descended from Italian, Maltese, Portuguese and Spanish settlers. Others are descended from British military personnel who were formally stationed there. Almost all I inhabitants live in apartments in the town of Gibraltar, and the workers are primarily employed by its government, by dockyards or in jobs related to the tourist industry.

As for the Rock itself, it is nearly 14,000 feet high and is located off the southwestern tip of Europe on the Iberian Peninsula. It is considered crown property of the United Kingdom, forms a peninsula that juts out into the Strait of Gibraltar and borders Spain.

Occupying nearly all of Gibraltar's 2.3 square miles, most of its uppermost area is covered by a nature reserve where about 250 Barbary macaques reside. These animals — the only wild population of monkeys in Europe — along with a labyrinthine network of tunnels — attract numerous tourists evet year. The underground tunnels are known as the Galleries and Great Siege Tunnels.

These underground tunnels have a unique history. They were first dug in the late 1700s. The British commander wanted to create the potential for cannon fire upon Spanish batteries in the area below the north face of the Rock. The siege lasted about four years, and during that span, the British constructed six such embrasures and mounted four cannons.

The so-called Galleries were constructed later on. Comprised of an entire system of halls, passages and embrasures nearly 1,000 feet long, they too are a popular tourist attraction. From that location, visitors are able to view the Bay of Gibraltar, the isthmus and Spain itself.

All told, the Rock contains over 100 caves. The most prominent and the most visited is St. Michael's Cave, situated halfway up the western slope of the Rock. Within it is another area called Cathedral Cave, once thought to be bottomless and therefore an underground link to Africa.This has never been substantiated.

Cathedral Cave now serves frequently as an auditorium for concerts, ballet and drama presentations. The beauty of its crystallized surroundings draws raves from the numerous attendees. They are particularly drawn to a centuries-old stalagmite that became so heavy it dropped and landed on its side at the far end of the chamber.

From a military standpoint, it was fortified by over 30,000 British soldiers and sailors during WWII, thus playing a key role in the defense of shipping routes in the Mediterranean. In 1942, during the war, the Allies launched an attack from

Gibraltar against German and Italian forces in North Africa. And as recently as 1997, it was revealed that Britain had concocted a secret plan to hide servicemen in the Rock's tunnels in case the Germans captured it. It was named "Operation Tracer" and had the radio capability to report all enemy movement. A six-man team remained undercover for over two years before they were disbanded and returned to civilian life.

Such a history of sieges and military action is responsible for the popular saying, "solid as the Rock of Gibraltar". Technically speaking, it is not based on the solidity of the Rock itself, rather on the action and dedication of the servicemen assigned to it.

# Chapter 14

## London's War Room

In London, not far from Scotland Yard, they took a short walk past Buckingham Palace and St. James Park. They were ready for the Cabinet War Rooms, located deeply underground and protected by a six-foot pad of steel and concrete.

Aided by a map with explanatory text, they began with the steel-beamed Cabinet Room where more than 100 meetings were held between 1940 and 1945. The critical importance of decisions and strategies arrived at in this subterranean chamber is belied by its Spartan simplicity There on the far side of a rectangular conference table is the prime minister's broad-backed chair, doughty and emblematic beneath the world map.

American visitors find themselves swallowing hard at the glass frontage of a cubicle, one of the most important facilities in the complex. The small bare room appears like a shrine-like setting for a black cult object — a cradle phone. Here was the ultimate in 1940's technology, a transatlantic hot line. From here, Churchill could speak directly by radio telephone to Franklin Roosevelt in Washington. On the wall to the right is a clock with black hands showing London time, red hands indicating Washington time.

Further down the corridor is the room where typists worked round the clock, breathing lightly of the vent-delivered air, often sleeping after late shifts in dormitories in the sub-basement.

Like all truly important museums, the War Room complex is more than a memorial and authentic setting of great events. It works in sounds, images and small telling events — the grim gas mask lying next to a shabby string purse spilling ration coupons; the quill pens and primitive little adding machines with tin flak helmets hung on pegs above them; the door to the Transatlantic Telephone Room with the special lock marked, "Vacant" and "Engaged" taken from a toilet door; the cloudy little hand mirror in the Mess Room hanging next to a poster advising: "Better Pot-luck with Churchill today than Humble-Pie under Hitler tomorrow. Don't waste food!"

They took in Churchill's bedroom, the War Room with a fan for his cigar smoke, the colossal map with its scattered pushpins, and an array of colorful phones nicknamed, "the beauty chorus".

In an article by David Knowles, we can read: "A 21-room time capsule beneath the former Office of Works building, these Cabinet War Rooms are a far better memorial to World War II than Europe's deserted battlefields. From here, Churchill directed the British campaign. You can almost hear his shoe leather slapping against the linoleum floor. Whenever you look in this bunker-turned-museum at the thousands of pinholes on a world map marking torpedo strikes, at the BBC microphone that the prime minister used to address the nation — the place simply resonates with the past".

And what stands out are his words: “Fill the armies, rule the air, pour out the munitions, strangle the U-boats, sweep the mines, plough the land, build the wounded, uplift the downcast, and honor the brave”.

# Chapter 15

## Pavarotti

Luciano Pavarotti is one of the greatest tenors of all time. His inimitable voice and charismatic personality, his passionate commitment to music, and his appetite for life have worked a particularly potent sort of magic. He has attracted millions throughout the world to an art form that was once regarded as the exclusive preserve of the privileged.

Opera was his passion and, since he was a man who needed to share his joys in life with other people, he committed himself throughout his career to making it as accessible to everyone as it was to him when he was young.

When he stood in the spotlight at the end of a solo concert, with a hundred thousand people still crying out for more, it is hard to comprehend that this was only a tiny fraction of his audience. Live television and radio broadcasts would be followed up by video, cassette and disc recordings to take his voice to millions more around the world.

In 1961, his career was just beginning, and fame beyond the narrow limits of the operatic world was almost inconceivable for anyone in his profession. His highest ambition was one day to play the tenor leads in international productions, but his individual blend of qualities and talent worked a particularly potent sort of alchemy. The fact that he succeeded in breaking all the rules and achieved infinitely more than he aspired to, was due in no small part to his personality.

Almost everyone knows that he was a big, warm-hearted Italian singer; that he loved to eat, and was crazy about football. To understand his success and why his voice stopped people in their tracks, one needs to appreciate how clearly he reflected his origins and to know the man himself a little better. Some of the missing pieces in the picture involve an image not only of a great tenor but of a man passionately committed to everything he did.

He was disciplined in his working life and childishly irrepressible in his capacity for having fun. He was generous and demanding, with close family relationships, impulsive shopping sprees, an exaggerated interest in his health and a love of people that he communicates to his many fans and to everyone he meets.

He owes his love of music — the force that motivates his life — to an operatic tradition that is firmly rooted in the region where he was born. It was Modena, a small northern Italian city. As well as being his home base, it was where all his deepest loyalties resided.

There will never be anyone else like him.

# Chapter 16

## Budapest

In December, 1992, Budapest celebrated its 120th birthday — the anniversary of Buda and Pest. But the metropolis on the Danube River can actually look back on 2,000 years of history. And it fast regained its splendor. Once the center of culture in the Austro-Hungarian Empire, the city and its buildings and treasures were neglected or damaged by a succession of invaders and occupiers. But with a democratic government in place since 1990 and a lengthy series of renovations, it has rebuilt many of its historic landmarks.

The capital of Hungary, Budapest, is the heartbeat of the country. In hilly Buda — on the Danube's west side — there is evidence of its political and imperial past, with the Royal Palace and the National Gallery situated there. It amounts to the history of the Hungarian people. Though Buda is marked both by defeats and victories, its national pride has never diminished.

On the east bank, there is Pest, the city's contemporary face, a thriving center of commerce and art — filled with cafes, restaurants, boutiques, and theaters.

The city-splitting Danube is an integral part of the city's life, not only in terms of its beauty, but also its vital use as a waterway for commerce and tourism. Three impressive bridges link the two sides: the Chain Bridge, Margret Bridge, and, at its narrowest point, the Elizabeth Bridge.

In its communist past — 1956 — the people of Budapest rebelled, demanding freedom of speech and social reform. Soviet troops quickly responded and crushed the rebellion in a matter of days.

In 1903, author Arthur Synons wrote: "In Budapest there is nothing but what the people and a natural brightness make of it. Here, things are what they seem; atmosphere is almost one of illusion. Budapest lives with a speed that thrusts itself, not unattractively, upon one at every moment. The people with their somber, fiery and irregular faces have the look of sleepy animals about to spring".

For those deciding to venture in Budapest there is a so-called Tourist Prayer worthy of being read:

Heavenly Father, look down at us, your humble, obedient tourist servants who are doomed to travel this earth, taking photographs, mailing postcards, buying souvenirs, and walking around in drip-dry underwear.

We beseech you, oh Lord, to see that our airplane is not hijacked, our luggage is not lost and our overweight baggage goes unnoticed.

Protect is from surly and unscrupulous taxi drivers, avaricious porters, and unlicensed English-speaking guides.

Give us this day divine guidance in the selection of our hotels that we might find our reservations honored, our rooms made up and hot water running from the faucets.

We pray that the telephones work and that the operators speak our tongue and that there is no mail waiting from our children that would force us to cancel the rest of our trip.

Lead us, dear Lord, to good, inexpensive restaurants where the food is superb, the waiters friendly and the wine included in the price of the meal.

Give us the wisdom to tip correctly in currencies we do not understand. Forgive us for under-tipping out of ignorance and over-tipping out of fear.

Make the natives love us for what we are and not for what we can contribute to their worldly goods.

Grant us the strength to visit the museums, the cathedrals, the palaces and the castles listed as MUSTS in the guidebooks.

And, perchance , we skip a historic moment to take a nap after lunch, have mercy on us, for our flesh is weak.

# Chapter 17

## Crime and Comedy Don't Mix

When you get beyond a certain age, comedy might lose its appeal. In fact, that's why there isn't as much of it on television these days. But even if there was, many wouldn't tune in because they're not interested in what's offered. What? Comedy with a racial twist? Or a political twist?

So the following represents that offered up to the 80s but not beyond then. The 50s, 60s, 70s and 80s? Yes. But beyond those years? No. And if you're trying to figure out what's with "Crime and Comedy Don't Mix", crime is not comedic and comedy is not criminal — and therein lies justification for such a title.

In the four decades mentioned, the types of comedy that prevailed were satire, parody, clowns, stand-up, slapstick, dead-pan, and so on. But listed will be a restriction to an overview of American Television Comedy. Most people would no doubt name the following characters as those who made them laugh the most:

— Bob Hope

— Jack Benny

— Milton Berle

— Sid Caesar

— Lucille Ball

— Red Skeleton

— Charlie Chaplin

— Carol Burnett

— Dick Van Dyke

— Henny Youngman

— Marty Feldman

And there were great teams:

— Burns and Allen

— Fibber McGee and Molly

— Dick Van Dyke and Mary Tyler Moore

— Carol Burnett, Harvey Korman and Tim Conway

— Abbott and Costello

Most people interviewed would probably indicate that the best comics in special categories were:

— Best stand-up: Hope and Benny (a tie)

— Best clown: Red Skeleton

— Best in sit-com: Lucille Ball

— Best satirist: Mort Sahl

Certain comics were identifiable by special traits or activities:

— Jack Benny as stingy, though he wasn't in real life

— Henny Youngman who loved his wife dearly but irreverence toward wives was "not in style".

— Rodney Dangerfield who had that shoulder tic

— Marty Feldman who had bug eyes that deviated

— Bob Hope who entertained military troops for years

Now to take personalities and shows in each of the decades:

— 50s:

— Jack Benny

— Milton Berle

— Sid Caesar

— Burns and Allen

— Victor Borge

— Ernie Kovacs

— Amos and Andy

— Our Miss Brooks

— Ozzie and Harriet

— The Life of Reilly

— Danny Thomas

— Phil Silvers

— George Gobel

— Jackie Gleason

— Red Skeleton

— Charlie Chaplin

— I Love Lucy

Speaking of the latter: "I Love Lucy" revolutionized the television industry with many innovations. It was the first TV program based in California instead of New York. It was the first program done on film rather than live — and kinescoped from a television screen. It was the first dramatic program ever to be done before a live studio audience and to be filmed in sequence, using the three camera technique. And it set the pattern for situation comedies for years to come. Henceforth, women would be scatterbrained but extremely clever; men would be loud and indignant; and friends would be dupes and accomplices.

Next, the 60s:

— Andy Griffith and Don Knotts

— Dick Van Dyke

— Bewitched

— Get Smart

— Hogan's Heroes

— Carol Burnett, Tim Conway and Harvey Korman

— The Smothers Brothers

— Laugh-In

— Rowan and Martin

70s:

— Mary Tyler Moore

— All in the Family

— Sonny and Cher Comedy Hour

— Mash

— Happy Days

— Dean Martin Show

— Flip Wilson Show

— Welcome Back, Kotter

— Laverne and Shirley

— Robin Williams

80s:

— Cheers

— Family Ties

— Bob Newhart

— The Love Boat

— The Cosby Show

— The Simpsons

— Seinfeld

That covers the last 40 years. Now a word or two about Benny and Hope. Benny was the one who always claimed he was 39-years-old. Here are a few snippets about him and his shows:

His stage character was a clever inversion of his actual self. The character was just about everything Benny was not: cheap, petty, vain, self-congratulatory. He was a master at it and these traits became the vital linchpin to the Benny shows' success. He set himself up as the comedic foil, allowing his supporting characters to draw laughs at the expense of his stinginess, vanity, and pettiness. Remember him standing there with his arms folded across his chest?

His supporting characters were the best in the business:

Mary Livingston, his wife and on-stage girlfriend

Announcer Don Wilson

Bandleader Phil Harris

Young tenor Dennis Day

Eddie Anderson as Rochester

Sheldon Leonard as a tight-lipped racetrack tout

Joseph Kearns as Ed. He guarded Jack's money vault and hadn't seen the light of day for decades.

Artie Auerbach as the Yiddish-accented Mr. Kitzel

And, of course, the versatile Mel Blanc who provided several characters' voices, like Polly the Parrot, or the railroad announcer with the never to be forgotten: "Train leaving on track five, for Anaheim, Azuza and Cucamonga"!

Benny's aging auto — his Maxwell

The perpetually frustrated violin teacher who was always on the verge of suicide because of Jack's abysmal playing.

Benny was also a master of the carefully timed, pregnant pause. Remember the "money or your life routine"? It produced one of the longest laughs in radio history. Benny was walking down a street and was accosted by a mugger. After asking for a match to light a cigarette, the mugger said, "Don't make a move. This is a stick-up. Now, come on — your money or your life". Benny paused and the audience howled. The mugger then repeated, "I said your money or your life". That's when Benny snapped back without a break: "I'm thinking! I'm thinking! This time the audience laughed louder and longer than they had during the pause.

Now, regarding Bob Hope. There's so much one can say about him: his comedy; entertaining the troops for so long; his golf; his movie road shows with Bing Crosby and Dorothy Lamour. It's been said that he became the most recognizable profile and talent in the world. In the entire history of show business, no individual has traveled so far — so often—to entertain so many.

He was born in England and once joked, "I left England at the age of four — when I found out I couldn't be king".

Again, superb support:

Jerry Colonna

Cobina Wright

Skinny Ellis and his orchestra

Les Brown and his Band of Renown

Announcer Bill Goodwin

Featured singers Judy Garland, Frances Langford, and Doris Day.

He received many, many honorary Oscars, 2,000 awards, and 54 honorary doctorates.

An avid golfer, he developed the Palm Springs Desert Classic. Once, in 1995, his foursome included President Bill Clinton, and former presidents George Bush and Gerald Ford. Afterwards, he said, "Clinton had the best score; Bush and Ford hit the most spectators; and I cheated better than ever".

And that wraps up crime and comedy. Remember: they just don't mix!

132 Jerry Labriola

# Chapter 18

## Marilyn Monroe

The world saw Marilyn as a sex symbol but underneath, she was an empowered woman. She was tough and smart, with a burning desire to lift herself up. But she had a burning vulnerability and, as the years passed, a palpable sadness about herself. She was usually difficult to work with and very unpredictable.

The word that seems best in describing her is, "tragic". Tragic childhood, tragic life, tragic death. But she was a working, striving person all her life — from coping with many close relatives who had serious mental illnesses and were institutionalized; and with an unhappy childhood of neglect, alleged sexual abuse and emotional heartache.

There was the enforced drudgery of orphanages and foster care; endless hours of factory work; modeling; and, from age 22 to 36, to being a highly emotional movie actress.

Her real name was Norma Jean Mortensen. Born in Los Angeles in 1926, she died in August, 1962. She was married and divorced three times: to James Dougharty at just under age sixteen; to baseball legend Joe DiMaggio; and to Famous playwright Arthur Miller.

She appeared 29 films, most notably:

— All About Eve

— Niagra

— Something's Got to Give

— How to Marry a Millionaire

— Gentlemen Prefer Blondes

— There's No Business Like Show Business

— The Seven Year Itch

— Some Like It Hot

— Bus Stop

— The Misfits

Drugs and alcohol were staples in her life—more so in the last year-and-a-half. She had several unsuccessful pregnancies; suffered from frequent bouts of depression; and attempted suicide four times.

She often commented on her unhappy childhood, saying, "The world around me then was kind of grim. I had to learn to pretend in order to — I don't know — to block the grimness. The whole world seemed sort of closed to me. I felt on the outside of everything and all I could do was to dream up any kind of pretend game".

Four key questions about her story are at once sensational and controversial:

— Was there a Kennedy connection?

— Was she considered a national security risk?

— Was there an organized crime connection?

— How did she die and was there a conspiracy involved?

A Kennedy connection? Most likely. She was often seen in the company of either John or Robert Kennedy. Peter Lawford, a Kennedy brother-in-law is frequently mentioned as a go-between. Speculation is that although she had sexual relations with them both, her heart was really with John. One her friends said she imagined herself as a future first lady.

You may recall her televised birthday tribute o the president four months before her death. It was in Madison Square Garden and was a very erotic performance as she breathlessly sang, “Happy Birthday”. It sent ripples of gossip around the world because her desire for John was probably displayed for the first time. Immediately after, the president hurried to the stage and chidingly thanked her for singing to him in ”such a sweet and wholesome way”.

Now the next three questions will be taken together: national security risk? Organized crime connection? A conspiratorial death? Along with the Kennedy connection, most sources answer “yes” to all four.

The world changed for a generation after the assassination of JFK — followed a few years later by the murder of brother Robert and of Martin Luther King. The strange prologue to these turning points was Marilyn’s death.

There are many FBI documents about Marilyn that have deletions and blacked-out passages. But many are marked, “internal security”. They detail three chapters of her life: meeting and marrying Miller; her post-marriage activities including meeting American communists in Mexico; and her high-stakes relationships with the Kennedy brothers until her death.

Writer and director Donald Wolfe sums things up best, “Marilyn Monroe was in a position to bring down the presidency. She was cognizant of Jack Kennedy’s marital infidelities and other private matters. She had his notes and letters and was privy to Kennedy's involvement with mobster Sam Giancana. That the Kennedy brothers had discussed national security matters with the film star added to an astonishing array of indiscretions".

Theories on the way she died? Suicide, accident or murder? A number of forensic experts have discarded the suicide theory. A rectal enema she administered to herself? C'mon. So, an accident? Probably not. Murder? If so, was she murdered by the Mafia, eager to avenge itself on the Kennedys' philandering to the American public? The motive was probably there but with what is known about the individuals present in her home on the night of August 4, 1962, it makes a mob hit with a rectal enema almost absurd.

Finally — some elaborating:

— No suicide note was ever recovered.

— Barbiturate tablets have entered the saga but how could she have swallowed any when no water glass was found near her and the plumbing system in her bathroom was not functioning?

— Why did it take four hours after the discovery of her body for the police to be informed?

— Her autopsy showed no residue tablets in her stomach or small intestine.

— She had a fresh bruise on her that could have resulted from violence.

— Purple discoloration of the large intestine suggested that drugs may have been introduced there.

— At the end, Peter Lawford stated that Marilyn had taken her last big enema.

# Chapter 19

## JFK Assassination

Shortly after noon on November 22, 1963, President John F. Kennedy was assassinated as he rode in a motorcade through Dealey Plaza in downtown Dallas, Texas.

By the fall of 1963, he and his political advisors were preparing for the next presidential campaign. At the end of September, the president traveled west, speaking in nine different states in less than a week. The trip was meant to put a spotlight on natural resources and conversation efforts. But he also used it to sound out themes—such as education, national security and world peace.

Arriving at Love Field in Dallas, he and his wife disembarked and immediately walked toward a fence where a crowd of well-wishers had gathered, and they spent several minutes shaking hands.

The procession left the airport and traveled along a ten-mile route that wound through downtown Dallas on the way to the Trade Mart where the president was scheduled to speak at a luncheon.

Crowds of excited people lined the streets and waved to the Kennedys. The car turned off Main Street at Dealey Plaza around 12:30 p.m. As it was passing the Texas School Book Depository, gunfire suddenly reverberated in the plaza.

Bullets struck the president's neck and head and he slumped over toward Mrs. Kennedy. Governor Connally was shot in his back.

The car sped off to Parkland Memorial Hospital just a few minutes away, but nothing could be done for the president. A

Catholic priest was summoned to administer the last rites and at 1:00 p.m. Kennedy was pronounced dead. Though seriously wounded, Governor Connally would recover.

The president's body was brought to Love Field and placed on Air Force One. Before the plane took off, a grim-faced Lyndon B. Johnson stood in its tight, crowded compartment and took the oath of office administered by U.S. District Court Judge Sarah Hughes. The brief ceremony took place at 2:38 p.m.

Less than an hour earlier, police had arrested Lee Harvey Oswald, a recently hired employee at the Depository. He was being held for the assassination of the president and for the fatal shooting—shortly afterward — of Patrolman J.D. Tippit on a Dallas street.

On Sunday morning, November 24, Oswald was scheduled to be transfered from police headquarters to the county jail. Viewers across America watching the live coverage suddenly saw a man aim a pistol at him and fire at point blank range. The assailant was identified as Jack Ruby, a local nightclub owner. Oswald died two hours later at Parkland Hospital.

That same day, the president' flag-draped casket was moved from the White House to a grave site. There, Mrs. Kennedy and her husband's brothers, Robert and Edward, lit an eternal flame.

Perhaps the most indelible images of the day were the salute to his father given by three-year-old John F. Kennedy, Jr., while his daughter Caroline knelt next to her mother at the president's bier. Extraordinary grace and dignity were shown by Jacqueline Kennedy.

As people throughout the nation and world struggled to make sense of a senseless act and to articulate their feelings about President Kennedy's life and legacy, many recalled these words from his inaugural address:

All this will not be finished in the first one hundred days, nor in the first one thousand days, nor in the life of this administration. Nor even perhaps in our lifetime on this planet. But let us begin.

Attention should be given to the so-called Zapruder film. It's a motion picture sequence shot by Abraham Zapruder as Kennedy's motorcade passed through the plaza. Unexpectedly, it ended up capturing the assassination. It gives a clear view from a somewhat elevated position on the side from which the president's fatal head wound is visible.

# Chapter 20

## Sacco-Vanzetti

Most people have never heard of Nicola Sacco and Bartolomeo Vanzetti. They were Italian anarchists charged with the 1920 killing of a shoe factory paymaster and his guard in South Braintree, Massachusetts. What follows will be an historical summary.

Their controversial trial is universally included among America's most famous, not only because of issues of ethnicity, draft evasion, radicalism and an arguably bigoted judicial system but also because of the passion of the times.

In the eyes of many, never in American legal history has public apprehension so shaped the outcome of a trial; never has one been conducted under such a shadow of ethnic hatred and political panic. And thrust in the middle of this landscape were two admitted radicals who embodied the twin threats of an unwelcome foreign element preaching a foreign political view.

World War I had just ended and political change was rampant abroad The Bolsheviks had final gained a foothold in Russia; a man named Hitler was advocating an anti-Semitic policy in Germany; the Austro-Hungarian Empire had been decimated; and the entire world appeared engulfed in a surging sea of socialism.

At home in America, an ailing Woodrow Wilson was president but would soon be succeeded by Warren Harding. Prohibition was in full force, sparking the boom of speakeasies, and F. Scott Fitzgerald wrote, "The uncertainties of 1919 were over. America was going on the greatest, gaudiest spree in history". Outwardly, there was little doubt that the country's mood and its aspirations were changing. The start of the decade found its youth turning into social desperadoes; daring, hard-drinking and cynical. Men mocked authority and flaunted their recklessness. Women's skirts were shorter while silk stockings and bobbed hair replaced hobble skirts and flowing tresses.

Those were the days of "giggle water" and "the cat's meow"; when a loaf of bread cost a dime and a pound of flour sold for less. People were caught up in Al Jolson, the Charleston and jazz; and they cheered loudly over Jack Dempsey in the boxing ring and Babe Ruth in the ballpark. All this was the veneer.

For in the face of the "Red Scare" or the rise of communism, the inner mood of the country was decidedly fearful. Unlike the Vietnam War nearly a half-century later, World War I was a popular conflict as Americans had rallied around Wilson's declaration that, "The world must be safe for democracy". Almost anyone who opposed the war, therefore, was looked upon with contempt.

Despite the finality of execution, this case has never achieved closure for it was cast from the beginning into a smoldering cauldron of judicial, scientific, political and social dispute. To this day, some people believe the trial and its aftermath — six years of legal wrangling — was a travesty of legal procedure. They feel the defendants were framed, that forensic evidence may have been tampered with, and that the police investigation was slipshod at best.

In some fictional stories, setting is stressed more than in others. Its purpose is to set the stage for the drama to follow, to anchor it in time and place. But only infrequently will such a design drive the action or otherwise influence it. Not so in the non-fictional saga of Sacco-Vanzetti. Rarely has the confluence of events — the Russian Revolution, the armistice, Red hysteria, patriotism, and journalism's focus on gangsterism — played on the emotions of an era's average citizen and on its movers and shakers alike: politicians, educators, the clergy, and all tiers of the criminal justice system. Like an unwanted foreign substance introduced into the bloodstream, Nicola Sacco and Bartolomeo Vanzetti happened upon the national scene at the wrong time.

So what had been fueled? The activities of peddlers of hate, of those advocating anti-Semitism and anti-Catholicism, such as the Ku Klux Klan. The result was that hatemongers and pro-American fever combined to produce increasingly more nasty groups who gained influence beneath a cloud of national distrust.

You know, there is so much to criticize about this case. A list of irregularities serves as a summary:

— Picking the jury. Those selected had to be in favor of the death penalty.

— Neither man owned a car, nor knew how to drive one. And important as some cars were in this case, how come this inexperience never came out?

— The police knew an important car was headed south. Why wasn't a roadblock set up? They could have phoned ahead.

— The important issue of Sacco's cap. It was allegedly found at one of the crime scenes. It was three sizes too small! Had it been planted? Chain of custody, alteration of evidence, false statements — if even there was a cap lying there in the first place. If not, it was found a day later and could have belonged to any employee going in and out of work.

— Four spent shells that were recovered from the crime scene. Three had a right twist. One, a left twist. Planted?

— The head of the Massachusetts State Police testified that they were guilty, but then changed his mind. Had there been collusion?

— Some bullets were also recovered from the crime scene. They and the spent shells changed hands many time over a period of a full year, plenty of time for a plant. A chain of custody issue.

— Nothing was done regarding fibers, hair, trace evidence, or shoe prints in a supposed getaway car or at the crime scene. Sloppy or deliberate?

— Several witnesses changed their testimony during and after the trial.

— The presiding judge was heard saying in public, ”They're obviously guilty. Let's prove it now”.

— Prejudicial trial issues. Each day, the defendants were marched to court from a nearby prison. They were handcuffed to each other, under heavy guard, and were led past crowds of people. In the courtroom, they were herded into an iron cage that was placed just before the bar — in full view of everyone, including the jury members.

After six years of appeals, they were executed.

# Chapter 21

## Talleyrand

Talleyrand (1754-1838) was a French statesman who was born into an aristocratic family in Paris. Witty, crafty and complex, he became one of the most controversial, influential and fascinating figures in French history. But his standing with the emperor was erratic at best.

Talleyrand's full name was Charles Maurice de Talleyrand-Perigord, Prince de Benevent. His clubfoot rendered him unable to enter a military career and marked him by his parents as unfit to carry on the family lineage. Early on, they stripped him of his birthright and any anticipated inheritance. Because he could not follow in the traditional military footsteps of the Talleyrand dukes, he embarked on a religious career, a move acceptable to his family and one which, they felt, would bring him some degree of social standing, at least.

At age sixteen, he began studies for holy orders at the seminary of St. Sulpice and nine year later received his degree from the Sorbonne and was ordained a priest.

He rose rapidly within ecclesiastical circles, combining both theological and political aspirations. But even during his student days, he exhibited a thinly veiled revolutionary philosophy. This eventually became more overt and after participating in activities considered radical by the Church (celebrating mass on the Champs de Mars to commemorate the anniversary of the storming of the Bastille; spearheading the confiscation of Church property for the national government), he was excommunicated in 1791.

Two years later, he fled to the United States after learning of a warrant for his arrest for unspecified charges. He spent three years in the Massachusetts area working in commodity trading and real estate speculation. The warrant was revoked in 1796 and he returned to France where, with the assistance of friends in high positions, he was appointed Foreign Affairs Minister of the ruling assembly.

At about this time, he caught the eye of Napoleon Bonaparte and, each man sensing the political merits of a friendship, they became allies. There followed a series of key political appointments granted by Napoleon between 1804 and 1814 including Grand Chamberlain and Vice-elector of the Empire; sovereign Prince of Benevento (a small principality taken from the Pope); and representative of France at the Congress of Erfurt.

But Talleyrand was also involved in some shady and sinister developments during this same period and his relationship with the emperor began to deteriorate. They were at odds on several military and foreign policy matters. Talleyrand publicly condemned what he called the crude treatment of Prussia. He opposed the Franco-Russian Alliance and, later, the attack on Russia. From 1812 on, he became a Russian secret agent. In effect, he became a spy for Russia, Austria and

England, accepting bribes from them to reveal Napoleon's secrets. He even demanded bribes from the United States. His firm stand against the Spanish campaign so infuriated Joseph Fouche, the head of Napoleon's secret police, that it helped convince the emperor that he was plotting against him. This provided the spark for Napoleon's famous depiction of Talleyrand as, "a piece of dung in a silk stocking".

Because of his perpetually shifting loyalties, especially during the French Revolution (1789-1799) — sometimes supporting the revolution, the empire, or the monarchy — historians continue to debate whether the man was a consummate diplomat who valued France's survival at any cost or a mercenary who selfishly sought out opportunities to "feather his own nest".

One thing was certain: he was a voluptuary who had a passion for sexual liaisons. It is said that he had four illegitimate children including the painter, Eugene Delacroix, and possibly one who was conceived while he lived in America. He was furthermore a gourmet and in early 1800, owned the elegant Chateau Haut-Brion in Bordeau. In this connection, he hired outstanding culinary personnel and was reputed to acquire only the finest tea and spices directly from the British East India Tea Company.

# Chapter 22

## Gens de Verite'

Leon Cassell was the longtime chairman of this French organization which had been in existence since the fall of Napoleon in 1815. It was a private group that worked alongside the French government but had never been part of it. When retained at a sizeable cost, it solved worldwide puzzles related to national security and defense initiatives of countries that sought its help. Even to scientific issues that would impact specific countries. Within France, it took up causes as the developed, focusing on projects lacking any iota of political or special interest rhetoric. Membership extended throughout Europe and numbered about two-thousand.

With regard to Leon himself, he'd had a distinguished career in law enforcement. Early on, he was a captain of both the police force and the Prefecture de Police in Paris. Ten years later, he taught criminology at their Grandes-Ecoles and, at the same time, lectured regularly at the Paris Museum. Currently he was teaching a course on Corrections, Crime and Criminology at what was once referred to as the Sorbonne and now as the University of Paris.

Scott had many times heard Leon explain that it was ironic for the original College de Sorbonne to be suppressed during the French Revolution only to be reopened by Napoleon in 1808, and that today the university has many colleges. He would stress that the "Sorbonne" had become a colloquial term for the entire collection. Then too, he was proud of a strong relationship with the British military. Thus, his background was full and varied.

Scott had been called upon to lead several of Verite's investigations and succeeded beyond expectations. Leon usually demanded more than Scott had been hired for, but Scott would remain tolerant because of Leon's relationship with Napoleon, a blood relationship based on DNA analysis.

Scott had never inquired about such a connection either because he was doubtful of it or because it sounded too serious for a mind that felt cluttered most of the time. In such situations as this, he declared the subject insignificant. But it would later become EXTREMELY significant in the overall scheme of things and would have a direct and strong bearing on Scott's next move.

Several years before, there was a huge—and complicated—series of discussions between him and Leon. They revolved around the French statesman, Charles Talleyrand; a certain Lady Beckett who was a top executive with the British East India Tea Company; and with one Sophie Bauer, a spinster from Brussels who, it was alleged, also had a DNA-based relationship with Napoleon.

In the first place, it was generally accepted that Lady Beckett was one of Napoleon's lovers, even while he was exiled on St. Helena. And it appeared that through the influence of the tea company and with Talleyrand's manipulations, she managed to see Napoleon on a regular basis.

In the second place, no one was convinced that the emperor was later murdered; or that he had succumbed to cancer as his father had; or that he died accidentally from arsenic inhaled from the colored wallpaper lining the walls of his sleeping quarters.

And in the third place, because of a poorly understood hypothesis, the possibility existed that Napoleon's body was not in a tomb at Paris' Hotel des Invalides after all, but had been transferred to what was termed, "Beckett Gardens".

The upshot of it all was that Scott, his suitcase in hand, and close friend, Charlie, went to the gardens, identified a resting place clearly identified as that of Beckett's lover, and dug down to a largely deteriorated coffin, some of it crumbled into dust.

Leon had arranged for a supervisor and three-man digging crew to accompany him to the gardens for an "inspection". The supervisor had raised questions about such a designation but was silenced and rewarded with in no uncertain money terms.

The cobblestone entry drive was bordered on both sides by stone pots on rock pedestals, pachysandra, rose geraniums, towering sycamores and plane trees. Far off in the distance were row upon row of gravestones in a sea of yellows and reds and blues of flowers that Scott couldn't identify. Fifty yards in, the supervisor pointed to Lady Beckett's headstone, off to the right. And it was there that Scott wanted to begin their inspection.

He dug an inch into the ground with his foot. Two inches. More as the dirt seemed less compact. Then he met solid resistance.

"Here," he said to the diggers. "Could you please dig around here?"

They complied and within the length of a shovel blade, there was a clang. Scott had never conceived of trying to differentiate between the clang of metal on old rock and the clang of metal on cement. But if he now to place a wager, he would pick cement.

He felt blotches come, asked the men to broaden the hole, grabbed a shovel excitedly from one of them and outlined a three-by-six foot rectangular area around it. Before they had completely dug out the space, Scott looked at Charlie and shouted, "Pay dirt! Excuse the pun."

He kneeled down and cleaned off a one-foot square cement block with his hand. It bore the following inscription:

Wait For Me, My Beloved

It Will Not Be Long

1840

Scott's words came quickly now, as did his movements — almost twitchy. "The coffin there," he said. "Can you — would you — open it? Your boss would give the go-ahead. I swear to it."

The bulkiest of the diggers started in and the other two followed suit. They used tarnished tools taken from a tarnished toolbox. It didn't take long: iron screws dangled from the coffin's rim.

Scott and Charlie's eyes stopped blinking as they beheld a mummified corpse before them. There were dirty cloth fragments over most of the wasted body; yellowed ornaments; medals; and two swords.

The corpse's skull had disarticulated from the rest of the body and laid at an awkward angle to the chest, the bones of which were riddled with pockmarks.

Silently, the three of them put on surgical gloves. Scott picked up the skull and with a penknife, scraped off a few bone fragments into a small glass container which he removed from his briefcase. He then carefully put them into his pocket, hoping they would yield some mitochondrial DNA, a type of genetic material he knew would not degrade for centuries. This in contrast to the usual nuclear DNA which degrades rather rapidly. The only problem he could imagine in relying on the mitochondrial type is that it is passed on from generation to generation only in the female line of the family. Plus he knew that Napoleon had no female heirs except possibly a child he had fathered with Lady Beckett. Scott realized he was in the middle of a roll because of the thought of that child and because it bore an alarming resemblance to children mechanically stratified and programmed. Scott was familiar with Huxley's "Brave New World".

This was neither of those, however, even though closer examination revealed a few grains of truth hidden in a sand pile of elaboration and unwarranted generalization. But that was the essence of his cerebral activity, and he let the roll continue with no intention of stopping it.

Whenever he thought of DNA, for example, he thought of genes. And whenever he thought of genes, he thought of having written about both of those hereditary elements in one of his books: "Genes are evolutionary glue, binding all life in a single history that dates back some 3.5 billion years — a history that is written in the language of nature's universal information molecule — DNA. It has certainly revolutionized forensic science. But we have to be very careful, because the information gleaned may not be the kind we'd want to share with everyone. People might, in fact, use it against you.

Scott could never recite such a paragraph word-for-word, but occasionally he'd render a quote for anyone who would listen. He was especially proud of "written in the language of nature's universal information molecule — DNA". And automatically, he equated DNA's being an information molecule with a definite possibility that the body was that of the great Napoleon.

Scott decided not to wait. He whipped out his cell phone and called Leon to pass on the news of their find. The reaction of Verite's president was more evident in his voice than in his words: breathless, loud, raspier than usual — ending with, "I just can't believe it!".

And Scott's voice was just as breathless: "There it is, Leon, right before us. An awful sight. An awful-looking casket; falling apart; the body deteriorated. My theory about the background? For now, I'll just say that the body was stolen in 1840 when it was supposed to be transferred to Paris. No doubt

Lady Beckett was behind it. I see Talleyrand's hand in it, too. She wanted Napoleon buried in her gardens and expected to join him there later. Now we have to prove it's definitely his body. The DNA business will take a few weeks in a case like this. Eventually, I'll work up a written report for you.

# Chapter 23

## Diamond Types

So-called “blood diamonds” are also called ‘hot diamonds’; ‘conflict diamonds’; or ‘war diamonds’. They’re terms used for diamonds mined in a war zone and sold to finance an insurgent or invading army’s war efforts or a warlord’s activity. They pertain to diamonds mined during fairly recent wars in Angola, Belgium and Sierra Leone. In the late 90s, Angola sold diamonds to finance a war with its own government. And that’s the kind of thing that happened during civil wars in these and other African countries.

Diamonds intensified civil wars by financing militaries and rebel militias, as recently as 2013, a civil war erupted in the Central African Republic with both sides fighting over the country's diamond resources. Thousands of people died and more than a million were displaced.

Past wars fueled by diamond considerations have taken almost four million lives. In fact, millions of people are still dealing with the consequences of wars like that: friends and family members lost; lives shattered—physical and emotional scars that will last for generations. It's a real nightmare and diamonds are in the middle of it.

There's a very famous diamond that was stolen. It's called the "Blue Baron", originated in Amsterdam, and was modeled after the legendary "Hope Diamond" now housed in the Smithsonian Institute. They claim that the Blue Baron's value was set at $80,000 per carat but no one's sure how big it is. Some believe it's cursed and the reason is simply this: anyone who publically announces he or she wants to buy it and also mentions — are you ready for this? — Napoleon's name at the same time — well, that person is murdered!

At last count, six people were found murdered, including two who are members of Verite'. Both lived in Amsterdam. One's a woman: Annie Snider. The other's Johan Wannamaker.

Many have asked, "Why don't those jerko countries deal in real money, not diamonds"? And the most common response has been: "Ancient tradition, I guess".

# Chapter 24

## Volterraio Castle

"Napoleon and Volterraio Castle" was one of Scott's published books.

He pulled down a copy from the nearest bookshelf and located the appropriate pages within seconds. He was astonished at what he recalled when he wrote the book, and wondered whether it was filled with approximations, especially the dialogue. He then proceeded to read the following:

The location of the castle was on the island of Elba — site of Napoleon's first exile. It was perched on the summit of a rocky cliff that amounted to a collection of massive boulders with no paths to climb, nor any shrubs to grab onto during any ascent.

He and his wife, Mary Ellen, along with his constant companion, Charlie Banks, hardly spoke during the 15-minute drive to the "rutted road". Charlie stopped the car and all three piled out. Mary Ellen began taking pictures.

From their vantage point, the castle was more imposing than Scott had anticipated. He thought it bizarre that the only vegetation was either dotted around their shoes or, as viewed against the morning's darkening clouds, clinging to the castle itself. Isolated blades of grass brushed against his ankles while the castle itself appeared smothered in green, brown and yellow, like a camouflaged fortress.

He knew its construction dated back to the 11th century's Pison period and that it had no doubt shrunk in size. Still it appeared indestructible to him and there were other words that swept through his mind: powerful, graceful, and dignified. Most of all: timeless.

He hadn't discussed it with the others, but Scott had every intention of inspecting the castle up close, to glance over an entire sea as the Tuscans had done to spot invading Saracen pirates; to see its underground tunnels firsthand; to walk along its walls much like Napoleon had two centuries ago, before the crumbling and erosion had begun.

He also wanted to observe the blackbirds he'd read about. They had been delivered there as a trick, and he understood their offspring still nested among the ruins. In the dim light, he could barely make out a few circling about. Theirs were the only sounds he heard. Much smaller than usual, they gave the illusion that the structure was bigger than it was, as viewed from far off by the French, the Turks, the Saracens or any other enemies. And who knows, he mused, perhaps they might stumble upon something left behind, something hidden centuries before and now exposed. The box that napoleon allegedly carried on his frequent trips there? And if so, what was in it?

He removed his sunglasses for it was growing darker by the minute. He then asked Mary Ellen to wait in the car and lock its doors.

"You ready?" he whispered to Charlie.

"If you are. What looks like a route to the top?"

Scott tweaked his chin. Let's check around," he said "You go that way and I'll go the opposite." He pointed to his left and right. "If you find a halfway decent approach, give me a holler, but not too loud. I'll do the same."

"Got it," Charlie said. Incidentally, why are we speaking so softly?"

"So we might hear echoes of Napoleon's voice. The rumor is that he routinely spoke out loud in Italian up there."

They both chuckled. As Charlie went off, Scott circled to the right. He passed giant rock after giant rock on his left side. Interspersed among them were formations that brought to mind the stalagmites of caves he had explored such as those at the Rock of Gibraltar. He stopped occasionally to survey possible routes to the castle up high and, after a bend in the road, he looked back and saw that their car was no longer visible. Up ahead, several boulders formed a mound nearer the gutted road, narrowing it some.

Then — what the!

Scott thought his heart would race out of control.

Twenty yards in front of them he saw three men leaning against the back of a black sedan. They straightened in unison, hands on hips, legs apart. Red hoods covered their heads. The eye and mouth slots were overly large, revealing dark skin and mustaches. All three moved slowly toward him.

What to do? Strike up a conversation? Say, “Excuse me?” He would have done so had they not been wearing hoods.

Suddenly he heard Charlie’s voice from behind and slightly hillside. He held a pistol in each hand. “Back off!” he screamed at the men. He leaped onto the road and swiftly positioned himself in front of Scott.

The men kept coming.

"Stop or else! I mean it!" Charlie's voice was louder and firmer as he straightened both arms out toward the hooded men, now ten yards away.

They stopped.

"Put your hands behind your head, all of you." Without taking his eyes off them, Charlie twisted his mouth to the side and said, "Show 'em, Scott, in case they don't understand."

Scott complied and the men followed suit.

"Now, one by one, take out your guns — I'm sure you have some — and throw them on the ground," Charlie continued. "And don't try anything funny. I've shot these pistols many times before. Shake your heads if you understand me."

They shook their heads and within seconds, five handguns lay on the road.

"You in the middle,"Charlie said, "only one gun?"

The man didn't respond. Charlie tipped his pistol in his direction and the man reached into his back pocket.

“Easy now,” Charlie said. The man flipped a small pearl-handled gun onto the road.

“Thank you, gentlemen. Now all of you — on the ground, face down. Hands behind your head.

They spoke for the first time, each saying, “Si.”

Charlie handed one of the guns to Scott and said, “Keep them covered. Every second.” He picked up the guns and hurled them far up the cliff, one at a time. He then walked over to their sedan and shot out its tires.

“Let’s go, Charlie said. “There’s enough room to turn our car around. And you guys? We’re walking backwards, so don’t dare get up until we’re out of sight. Get it?”

As they inched away, Scott remained stunned over Charlie’s skill in taking control of the situation.

“Why didn’t you whisper to me that you’d be doubling back?” Scott asked.

"Because I figured if we were somehow being watched, he or they would notice and I didn't want them to. Besides, it wasn't necessary for you to know."

At the car, Mary Ellen bolted out. "I was so worried. I didn't know what to do. There were four shots. What happened?"

"Nothing," Charlie said, "Just testing my pistol."

They got into the car, Mary Ellen in back. Charlie maneuvered the car around and they sped off through a heavy but fleeting rain. It reminded Scott of his boyhood vacations in Florida.

"So you carry a gun, Charlie?" Mary Ellen asked in disbelief. "Around here? For sure."

"Back in Paris, you don't seem like the gun type."

"But away from Paris, I can even swallow swords."

"If you don't mind, let's level with her," Scott chimed in.

Charlie's expression didn't register disapproval so Scott explained what had transpired, ending with, "Let's get out of here fast and I don't mean this place. I mean the whole damn island. Screw it!"

# Chapter 25

## The Hague and Milosevic

The imposing International Criminal Court Building in the Hague could be seen as six connected structures with a garden motif. The tallest had a green façade, was placed in the center of the design, and was named the "Court Tower." It contained three courtrooms.

Scott parked near the Court Tower. He and Charlie entered it and headed in the direction of one of the courtrooms. By chance, they arrived in time to hear Knute Larsen, from the Office of the Prosecutor, introduce himself to a legion of tourists. Then he spoke of Baltic history and about Slobodan Milosevic, the so-called "Butcher of the Balkans." He said that the days involving the republics and provinces in that region were almost inconceivable.

It then continued on with his giving a half-hour of particulars about Slovenia, Bosnia-Herzegovina, Montenegro, Macedonia, and Serbia, including the autonomous province called Kosovo. He spoke of The Hague; so-called "ethnic cleansing"; the Balkan's history during both World Wars; and NATO's bombing of military targets throughout the Yugoslavia area.

Then, nearly another half hour on the establishment of an Independent State of Croatia by the Axis powers of Germany, Italy, Hungary and Bulgaria. These countries, he said, became a Nazi puppet state that soon created concentration camps for anti-fascists, communists, Serbs, Jews and gypsies.

"So-called Chetniks arose and they became allies of the United States in Europe, and the communist Yugoslav National Liberation Army led by Josip Tito. At first, the Chetniks were successful in widespread guerrilla warfare, but the Germans countered, the results totaling 1.7 million casualties."

But his main focus was on Milosevic, a dictator who, he said, orchestrated atrocities beyond belief — atrocities that resulted in the deaths/or brutalities of millions of people. Forced deportation of women, children and old men was highlighted, as were the burned bodies and mass graves of fighting-age men.

During a decade of violence and terror, he continued, many felt that the dictator's basic motivation amounted to a search for power. Power that was augmented by condoning the use of trucks containing bodies either packed upright or lying horizontally.

Scott cringed and, with eyes that became pinpoints of fire, he fought off an urge to rise up and demand that the Prosecutor discontinue the talk, and to complain: "My head is reeling; such splitting of territories; such savagery — hard to conceive it all."

Milosevic underwent a four-year-long trial and was not completed because he died of a heart attack.

# Chapter 26

## Cafés in Paris

The first café in the Western World was in Paris — established in 1686. The French had just discovered coffee, and their robust economy was growing a population of pleasure-seekers and thinkers looking for places to be seen, to exchange ideas, and to plot revolutions — both political and philosophical. With the advent of theaters, like the Comedie Francaise, the necessary artsy, coffee-sipping crowds bloomed in number. By 1700, more than 300 cafés had opened their doors. And at the time of the Revolution (1789), there were over 1,800 Revolutionaries from Napoleon to Salvador Dali enjoyed the spirit of free-thinking times that the cafe's engendered.

Café society took off in the early 1900s. life was changing rapidly as new technologies and wars appeared on a global scale. Many retreated to Parisian cafés to try to make sense of the confusion. Vladimir Lenin, Leon Trotsky, Igor Stravinsky, Ernest Hemingway, F. Scott Fitzgerald, James Joyce, Albert Einstein, Jean-Paul Sartre, Gene Openshaw, and Albert Camus were among the devoted café society visitors.

Some virtually lived at their favorite café where they kept their business calendars, entertained friends, and ate every meal.

There are more than 12,000 cafés in Paris today though their numbers are shrinking. But they're still used for business meetings, encounter sessions, political discussions and romantic interludes. Most Parisians are loyal to their favorites and know their waiter's children's names.

# Chapter 27

## Mystery Books

At the risk of sounding over-instructive, the following is offered:

In writing a mystery novel, do remember that a crime must be committed. It must be a significant one and the solution must not be stumbled upon. So, elaborate.

The hero must sweat. If he or she isn't in trouble, the book is. And don't tailor your challenges to your hero's strengths. Real growth through the course of a novel occurs when overcoming weaknesses, not just utilizing strengths alone.

Introduce the villain early, and spend as much time on the villain's motives as the hero's. In effect, the hero reacts to the villain — or potential villain — which means that such a person is the motor of the plot. It's a balancing act, really.

Suspects are cheap, so have enough. Five or six is a good number. If the crime is murder, pick a victim worth killing. This means several people should have motive, opportunity and means.

Let your characters impact the plot, not the reverse. Put another way: novels should be character driven. And don't force your characters to act out of character simply to further plot ends.

Have your characters act, not be acted upon. In this regard, nobody loves a villain, and there are reasons why protagonists are called heroes. Basically, they're loved. Villains are not. The well-known axiom, "Show, don't tell", enters the picture here. In other words, show the character deserving love — and the villain not deserving it. Not just telling about it.

Now, paragraph frequently in tense scenes. If not overused, one-sentence paragraphs can pack a lot of punch.

And shorten chapters for effect. Witness the late Robert Parker's writings.

Avoid generics — go for specifics. Don't let characters walk streets and drive cars. They should walk along Park Avenue looking for their Hondas. Mysteries revolve around details.

Use proper official procedures. Don't trade plot convenience for reader credibility. Do your homework.

Pile on the puzzles. One isn't enough — subplots can give your mystery texture and can provide a counterpoint for the main plot. In other words, they set it off by contrast.

Remember, everyone has something to hide. A seemingly straightforward murder can uncover an entire spider's web of suspicion. In your book, everybody who would have killed the victim is a little guilty — the killer just got there first!

Disguise, rather than withhold crucial information. All clues discovered by the hero must be made available to the reader. In other words, fair play. Readers need to see the pivotal clues without realizing what they're reading. Solving a mystery using withheld information is cheating the reader.

Use plot twists to add surprise. But not out of the blue. A plot twist works best if it's an unexpected change on the elements already presented in the plot. For instance, an investigation eventually determines that a victim's companion on an ocean cruise was not the person listed on a confirmation document, but someone else.

So what's been touched upon are:

— mystery requirements

— the victim

— the hero

— the villain

— suspects

— other characters

— show, don't tell

— suspense seeds

— shortened paragraphs and chapters in tense scenes

— specifics, not generics

— addled puzzles

— disguised information

— plot twists

# Chapter 28

## Forensic Science

What is it? The most concise definition is that it's the application of biological, chemical and physical sciences to matters involving the law. What is applicable here is a quote from Sir Arthur Conan Doyle's first novel, "A Study in Scarlet", written in 1887.

"I've found it. I've found it," he shouted to my companion, running toward us with a test tube in his hand. I've found a reagent which is precipitated by hemoglobin and by nothing else. Why, man — it is the most practical medico-legal discovery for years. Don't you see that it gives us an infallible test for blood stains? Now, this appears to act well whether the blood is old or new. Had this test been invented, there are hundreds of men now walking the earth who would long ago have paid the penalty for their crimes. A man is suspected of a crime months after it has been committed. His clothes are examined and stains discovered upon them. Are they blood stains, or rust stains, or fruit stains, or what are they? That's a question that has puzzled many an expert, and why? Because there was no reliable test. Now we have the Sherlock Holmes test, and there will be no longer any difficulty."

Simply amazing! That was many, many years ago!

There was a time when it and criminalistics were considered one and the same. But not any more. It's sort of an oxymoron, but the science has both expanded and contracted. Expanded in terms of bringing more disciplines under its umbrella, and contracted in terms of specialization — much like what's taken place in medicine.

So — imagine forensic science as an open umbrella. Down its center is a pole — its core. It is still criminalistics or criminology. What is it? It deals with crime scenes. With the recognition, collection, identification, preservation and interpretation of physical evidence at crime scenes. It also includes crime scene reconstruction. And at the bottom of that center pole are offshoots or subdivisions like:

— DNA analysis

— latent fingerprint analysis

— questioned document analysis such as ransom notes

— ballistics

— drug analysis

— voice analysis

— data banks for fingerprints, DNA, tool marks, tire marks and spent shells

— artificial intelligence involving crime mapping (which is how crime spreads), criminal profiling, crime scene reasoning and logic (that is, getting into the mind of a criminal)

Now then, off to the side of this center pole are many other poles that are squeezed into our depiction. In fact, just name any field, put the word "forensic" in front of it, and it now exists:

— forensic medicine

— forensic odontology

— forensic anthropology (skeletal remains)

— Forensic entomology (life cycle of insects to pinpoint time of death)

— forensic engineering

— forensic nursing

— forensic photography

— forensic accounting, for heaven's sake (blue collar crime)

# Chapter 29

## Jack the Ripper

An essay I wrote about him:

The time: a nine-week period in the fall of 1888.

The place: the Whitechapel district of London. That was the east end. Where the slums were. Where prostitutes flourished.

Few names in history are as instantly recognizable. Fewer still evoke such vivid images: noisy courts and alleys, cabs and gaslights, swirling fog, prostitutes decked out in the tawdriest of finery, the shrill cry of newsboys — and silent, cruel death personified in the cape-shrouded figure of a faceless prowler of the night, armed with a long knife and a Gladstone bag.

And his identity is still unknown — although there's hardly a year in the many years since, when a new brainstorm doesn't emerge. When experts don't continue to speculate.

There are many aspects to this saga:

— the homicides themselves, at least five, usually with horrible brutalization

— the victims, all prostitutes, usually older, and with alcohol problems

— the investigation — intense, prolonged

— the endless theories

— the abundance of graffiti

— the varied letters and postcards — some considered sent by the killer, but most considered hoaxes

— the suspects: a mad doctor, a professional butcher, a deranged mid-wife, a mysterious lodger, even a member of royalty.

Actually, so much of the Ripper is mired in mystery and myth. And

with the passage of time, much can get (1) exaggerated, (2) embellished upon, or (3) otherwise distorted.

Think of it this way: "The older the story, the more grains of salt it should be taken with."

To continue: why are there still stories and songs and operas and movies and a never ending stream of books about this one Victorian criminal? Why is the Ripper story as popular today as it was in Victorian London? For two main reasons: First, because Jack the Ripper represents the classic whodunit. The story has a terrifying, almost supernatural quality. It's been said that he came out of the fog, killed violently by slashing a throat from ear to ear, and quickly disappeared without a trace. And after his victim was found, he vanished from the face of the earth. Forever.

But over time, much has been distorted. And that brings us to the second reason for its continued fascination: misimpression. In spite of their barbarism, the murders represent a real-life mystery from the era of Sherlock Holmes — the late 1800s — the bygone, romantic era of high Victorian society, with gaslights and swirling London fog.

BUT GET THIS! NOT ONE SINGLE KILLING TOOK PLACE ON A FOGGY NIGHT! NOT ONE SINGLE KILLING HAD ANY REAL RELATIONSHIP TO VICTORIAN SPLENDOR!

There must be an unabashed claim that if DNA and the New Genetics — that is, modern forensic science — had been available back then, the mystery would have been cracked in short order. But just imagine — if that had been the case, we probably wouldn't have such a lasting melodrama, would we?

# Chapter 30

## Lisbon

This capital of Portugal lies on seven low hills at the estuary of the river Tagus, six miles from the Atlantic Ocean. It is on the west coast of Portugal with the Algarve to the south and Costa de Prata and Costa Verde to the north. The Estoril coast runs along the mouth of the Tagus Estuary on to the Atlantic as far as Ericeira.

The origins of Lisbon are shrouded in legend. Among its mythical boundries are Eliisha and Ulysses. It was occupied successively by Phoenicians around 1200 B.C., followed by the

Greeks, Carthaginians, Romans, Visigoths , Moors and was finally conquered in 1147 by Portugal's first king with the aid of English crusaders.

As the country developed, it became the greatest maritime power of the 15$^{th}$ century onwards. It became a very important world trade center in spices and jewels from the east, and gold from Brazil. Today, Lisbon is a lively, international city with a population of one-and-a-half million, and offers a combination of the old character plus a beauty all its own.

Its Albufeira features zillions of cork trees and blossoming olive trees which dominate the Algarve section in the winter. Club Albufeira is a sprawling complex some distance from the ocean. All the buildings in the immediate vicinity are white in color.

The city is proud of the Castle of St. George because of its location for amazing views of the city proper. Other places to visit are a huge monastery, a museum of carriages, a suspension bridge, very large statues of Christ and St. Anthony and Lisbon Cathedral with a diorama of Bethlehem.

You'll find rows of people waiting to read a tree poem embedded in a wooden plaque. Some who already read it have eased away with tears in their eyes:

You who walks by and at me, do raise your arm, and before you do me harm, look good at me.

I am the warmth of your home in the cold winter nights.

I am the friendly shade that you find when walking under the August sun and my fruits are pleasantly appetizing that they quench your thirst in these paths.

I am the friendly beam in your home, the board of your table, the bed where you rest, the wood of your boat.

I am the handle of your hoe, the door of your home, the wood of your crib and of your future coffin.

I am the bread of kindness and a rose of beauty. You that walks by, take a good look at me but don't do me any harm.

# Epilogue

That's it! Some kind of journey, eh?

If it's to be repeated, Mary Ellen and I invite you to join us.

They say, "One for the Ages." Well, this was, "One for the Pages."